The Happy Hollisters™
at Mystery Mountain

BY JERRY WEST

Illustrated by Helen S. Hamilton

D0188077

THE SVENSON GROUP, INC.
on behalf of The Hollister Family Properties Trust

Jacket copy from the original hardcover book:

While returning from New Mexico to the airport in their rented bus, the Hollister children stop to buy cowboy suits. Mr. Hollister, with an eye for items to sell in his store, The Trading Post, discovers the suits are designed by Marie Vega, the wife of an old college friend. Mr. Hollister contacts the Vegas and the whole Hollister family is invited to spend a few weeks on the Vega ranch.

Meanwhile, the children have met Helen and Jack Moore, youngsters about Pete's age, who are staying at a dude ranch not far from the Vegas' and Mystery Mountain. Jack has a map that leads to the cave of the ancient doll makers, the long buried secret of the mountain. Complications set in, however, when the Hollisters and the Moores meet the boy Willie and his friend the mysterious Mesquite Mike. Not only does the map disappear, but word is around that a rustler is taking sheep from the ranchers in the area.

Here is another exciting Hollister adventure. What happens to the children when they spend a night on the desert? Is there really a monster in Mystery Mountain? And who could the rustler be? All these questions are answered in this fast-moving story.

ISBN: 1-4636-5823-0

ISBN-13: 9781463658236

Dedication

The Happy Hollisters at Mystery Mountain is Volume 5 in a 33-book series. The books are being reissued in honor of my grandfather, Andrew Edward Svenson, who began *The Happy Hollisters* series in 1953 using the pseudonym Jerry West. The characters in the Hollister family were based in part on his family – my grandmother, father, uncle, and aunts – and I am grateful to them for inspiring these books, and for their support of this labor of love:

Marian S. Svenson – "Elaine Hollister"
Andrew E. Svenson, Jr. – "Pete"
Laura Svenson Schnell – "Pam"
Eric R. Svenson, Sr. – "Ricky"
Jane Svenson Kossmann – "Holly"
Eileen Svenson de Zayas and Ingrid Svenson Herdman – "Sue"

I am also grateful to my wife, Callie Larew Svenson,
for her diligent research and fastidious attention to detail
in preparing the manuscripts for reissue; and to my daughter,
Libby Svenson, for her creative energy and boundless
enthusiasm for this project.

Andrew E. Svenson III
The Svenson Group, Inc.
on behalf of The Hollister Family Properties Trust

"I love mountains," Pam said dreamily.
"And they always seem so mysterious . . ."

Contents

CHAPTER 1

"Ride 'em, Cowboy!"

"YIPPEE!"

"Can't catch me!"

The five Hollister children were playing cowboys and Indians in a little grove of cottonwood trees next to the motel where they had stayed overnight.

"I'm a cowboy girl!" shouted four-year-old Sue excitedly.

The dark-haired little girl was the only one wearing a Western outfit and looked very pretty in the white buckskin jacket and skirt trimmed with rabbit fur. It had been a gift that very morning from kind Mrs. Troy, who ran the motel, and the suit had inspired the game the children were playing.

"Holly, hide with me," Sue begged. "And don't let your pigtails give us away."

Her six-year-old sister giggled. Several times when they had played hide-and-seek Holly's long pigtails had hung out and given away her hiding place. She pulled them around her neck.

"Here comes Indian Ricky!" Holly reported. "Goody, he didn't see us!"

"Here comes Indian Ricky."

Ricky gave a loud war whoop and dashed past. He was seven, had reddish hair and a freckled nose. Right behind him was Pete Hollister, a tall, blond boy of twelve with a crew cut. At this moment his eyes were darting from left to right as he tried to find his three sisters.

Sue and Holly huddled together behind the big tree, but it was no use. Pete spied them.

"You're Big Chief Pete's prisoners!" he announced in a deep voice.

"Bet you can't find Pam," Holly dared him.

Pete did not find his sister Pam. But Ricky did, after a chase round and round among the trees and boulders. Pam was a good runner, but finally she stumbled and fell. Then he caught her.

Pam's pretty face was flushed and her golden hair was damp from the exertion of running. "I guess we'd better go back now," the serious ten-year-old girl said. "Dad and Mother are probably ready to leave."

The Hollister family had been on a trip to New Mexico and were now on their way back to the airport, where they would fly to their home in the East. They had tried to rent a large car for sight-seeing, but the only thing Mr. Hollister had been able to get was a school bus. What fun they had had in it, looking for a lost Indian treasure!

A horn began to toot loudly and the children scampered to the bus. Mr. Hollister, seeing Sue in her new cowgirl clothes, said:

"Well, my little daughter has gone Western!"

Sue glanced up into her tall, athletic-looking father's tanned face. "Please, Daddy, can't we stay here with the Mexicoses?" she asked.

He laughed, saying they would come back sometime. Right now he could not be away from business much longer.

"But I *would* stay in New Mexico a little while," he said, "if I could find some suits to buy like the one you have on. I'm sure I could sell a good many of them at the Trading Post." The Trading Post was Mr. Hollister's combination hardware, toy, and sporting-goods store in Shoreham, where the family lived.

Suddenly he leaned over and looked inside the collar of Sue's jacket, saying, "I wonder if the maker's label is sewed in. Yes, here it is. Hm. This is interesting."

"Hm, this is an interesting tag."

"What's int'restin'?" Sue asked, squirming because her daddy's finger tickled.

"This tag says *Maria Vega Clothes*. I had a friend in college named Frank Vega. He came from New Mexico, and I think he married a woman named Maria."

"Yikes!" Ricky shouted. "We can go see them and then we won't have to leave the West so soon!"

At this all the other children shouted, "Oh, Dad, could we?"

Mr. Hollister laughed. "I'll tell you what. If I can locate Frank Vega, I'll phone him and see what he says."

At this moment Mrs. Hollister came from the motel with Mrs. Troy. Immediately Ricky told her of the possible new plan. She looked at her husband and smiled. The children, who adored their gay, charming mother, knew from this that she approved.

"I do hope that you can find him," she said. "Have you any idea where the Vegas are?"

"No, but I believe Mrs. Troy can give us a clue," Mr. Hollister replied. Turning to the motel owner, he asked, "Would you mind telling me where you bought the outfit you gave Sue? Surely the store would have the Vegas' address."

"You won't have to go far to find out," Mrs. Troy said. "I bought the little cowgirl suit at the general store in Sunrise. That's only a few miles from here in the direction you're heading."

Excitedly the children climbed into the bus, each one in turn thanking Mrs. Troy for the good time they had had.

"It was very pleasant entertaining the Happy Hollisters," she called. "Have a good trip!"

Away the bus went down the road. It was a beautiful clear morning, and the faraway mountains seemed much closer than they really were.

"I love mountains," Pam said dreamily. "And they always seem so mysterious. Full of all kinds of strange flowers and animals."

"Some are," Pete replied. "But other mountains have nothing but rocks and are hard to climb."

"That's true," said Mrs. Hollister. "And still others are always covered with ice and snow."

"But I like the ones best," Holly spoke up, "that have tall trees and brooks."

They reached the little town of Sunrise.

After a half hour's drive across the rolling countryside dotted with various shapes and sizes of cactus
plants, the bus reached the little town of Sunrise. In the
center of it was a plaza with shade trees and benches
here and there. Surrounding the plaza were low flat-
roofed shops and houses, some white, some yellow, and
still others bright blue.

"I see the general store!" Holly called out. "Over
there, Dad!"

Mr. Hollister drove around the plaza to the far side
and parked in front of the shop. As he went inside to
inquire about the Vegas, Mrs. Hollister and the children looked in the display windows.

"Yikes!" Ricky cried. "There's a suit like Sue's, only
it has pants. Mother, do you think maybe I could have
that?"

"We'll go inside and price it," Mrs. Hollister replied. "How would you all like rabbit-furred suits if they don't cost too much?"

The cries of glee that followed her question were so loud that Mrs. Hollister clapped her hands over her ears. Ricky raced into the shop ahead of the others and was met by a short, bald-headed man.

"Howdy," he greeted the boy with a smile. "And what can I do for you?"

"My brother and three sisters—they're coming in—want cowboy outfits—"

"With rabbit fur, please," Holly interrupted, running up to Ricky. "But they mustn't cost too much."

"Well, now," the man drawled, "we need more cowboys out this way to catch the rustlers!"

Before the children could ask whether he was joking or not, the man added, "Seeing that you might buy four outfits all at once, maybe I could give you a special price. That's what I did for those folks over there."

The children looked across the store to where a thoughtful-looking girl of thirteen and a jolly boy of twelve were admiring themselves in a long mirror. Both had on the rabbit-trimmed Western clothes. The shopkeeper explained that the children's parents had bought two sets for some cousins as well as for their own son and daughter.

"Suppose you try on the outfits and see how you look in them," the man proposed.

He said something in a low voice to Mrs. Hollister. She nodded, replying that the price would be all right.

They found the rack of suits.

The children had already found the rack of suits and now picked out their right sizes. By the time Mr. Hollister returned to his family from an office at the back of the shop, they had them on.

"Am I seeing things," he said, laughing, "or have all my children turned into cowboys?"

"We're all dressed for life on the ranch, Dad," Pete answered.

"What did you find out about your college friend?" Mrs. Hollister asked.

"I believe I've located him," her husband replied. "The phone operator is trying to get his ranch now."

All this while the two strange children in the shop had been watching the Hollisters. Now they came over and the boy said:

"Are you going to a ranch? My sister and I are—to Bishop's Dude Ranch."

"We hope we're going to Mr. Vega's," Pete told him, and introduced his family.

Then the other boy said, "My name's Jack Moore. This is my sister Helen. Mother and Dad are at the hotel. They're coming for us in a little while."

Holly had an idea. "While we're waiting, let's all play out on the plaza in our new suits. May we, Mother?"

"All right. And, Pam, keep track of Sue."

"I will." Pam took hold of her sister's hand as they went outside.

"Hey!" cried Ricky, who was in front of them. He pointed to a cart at one side of the plaza under a tree. "What a funny old wagon!"

The girls paused to look at the odd cart, which had two huge wheels.

"I think it's an oxcart," said Pam.

"Let's ride in it," Ricky proposed excitedly, starting to climb up. "We'll take turns being oxen!"

"No, don't do that," Pam spoke up. "The sign says, *Don't touch.*" She read the inscription aloud:

"*This carreta was used by Spanish settlers who came to Sunrise in 1660.*"

"Pretty old," Helen said. "Imagine how valuable it must be!"

The children were very impressed as each thought of the oxcart being used almost three hundred years ago—maybe right where they were standing!

Ricky immediately made himself a promise. He would build an oxcart just like this one as soon as he got home.

"Only mine'll be brand new and won't fall apart," he was thinking. "Then everybody can ride in it instead of just looking!"

Pete and Jack had walked on ahead, looking for a good spot to play. Jack was saying, "I wish you were coming to Bishop's Ranch. Then you could help us solve the mystery."

"A mystery on your ranch?" Pete asked eagerly.

"Well, yes and no," Jack answered. "It's on a mountain, really. I'll tell you about it later," he said as Ricky called out, "Everybody ready for the game. Let's play 'Ride 'em, cowboy!' "

At once all the children posed as if they were on horseback. Then they began to "ride," slow, fast, jumping, twisting, and turning.

"Whoa!" Ricky shouted. "My pony's sun-fishing!"

The boy fell off. In his mad dash to catch the imaginary runaway horse and get out of the way of the other horses, he ran full-tilt into one of the wheels of the *carreta*. It dropped off with a loud *plop*, and one side of the cart fell to the ground.

"Oh, Ricky!" Holly cried, jumping off her make-believe horse. "You—you've broken it!"

Soon all the children were crowding around the tilted *carreta*. Pete and Jack began to examine it. Finally Pete said:

Pete slipped the wheel on.

"I think we can repair it. There's a wooden pin that goes through the hub. It fell out. Everybody help lift the axle and I'll try to fit the wheel back on."

All but Sue put their hands and shoulders to the ancient oxcart. Then as Pete gave the signal, they raised the end of the axle that lay on the ground. When it was high enough Pete slipped the wheel on and replaced the loose wooden pin.

"Good work," said Jack, and Helen added, "We'd better play on the other side of the plaza."

"Let's change to hide-'n'-seek," Sue proposed. "My pony's getting my cowboy girl suit all dirty."

"All right," said Pam. "I'll be *it* first."

The children scattered in all directions. Holly decided to make it hard for Pam to find her. None of the others noticed her as she dashed off toward the general store. Holly had seen two large cartons standing just inside the door and knew one was empty. Quickly she climbed inside it, pulling the open end closed.

"They'll never find me here." She giggled softly in the darkness and fingered her pigtails.

Holly could hear people going in and out of the store and finally Pete's voice shouting, "Come on in home free, Holly! We can't find you. We give up!"

"I'll let them guess a little while longer," Holly thought mischievously, and remained very quiet.

A few minutes went by and the little girl was just about to get out of the box when she heard footsteps approaching. They stopped right next to her hiding place. Now she certainly would be found! Holly held her breath and listened as hands touched the top of the carton.

"You're getting warmer!" Holly thought. "If you'll just open the top, you'll see me!"

But to her surprise, the top of the carton was not opened. Instead, the little crack of light that had shown through was suddenly blacked out entirely.

"Maybe it's Pete and he's teasing me," Holly reasoned.

To her amazement, she felt the box being lifted up.

"Oh, I'm being carried to the plaza to make the game more fun," Holly told herself.

Suddenly she became puzzled because she could hear only one pair of feet. Pete was strong, but not strong enough to carry the big box alone.

"I know!" Holly thought, smiling. "It's Daddy. I'll bet he's taking me right back to the bus."

The next second she received a hard bump. Whoever was carrying the box had let it down too fast. But Holly would be a good sport and not say anything.

"Now I'll pop out like a jack-in-the-box," she resolved, and pushed her head up against the top of the carton.

But the cover would not budge! And when she ran a finger along the edge of the cardboard lid, Holly found it had been fastened with strong tape!

"Oh dear," she gulped. "This isn't a very funny game any more."

Next she heard the rumble of a motor, and it was not the motor of the bus. The little girl felt herself moving! Her heart pounding with fright, Holly cried as loudly as she could:

"Help! Help! Let me out!"

"Help! Help!" cried the girl in the box.

CHAPTER 2

A Big Surprise

EVEN though Holly shouted again and again and thumped on the cardboard sides of the box with her fists, nobody came to free her.

"What'll I do?" Holly thought. She could not keep the tears from trickling down her cheeks.

As the minutes passed the truck drove steadily along. The little girl wondered where it was taking her and how soon the driver would find out his mistake.

All at once the unhappy girl felt the truck slow down. Then it swerved, as if making a turn, and at last came to a stop.

From outside came gleeful shouts of children, and Holly forgot her tears. She must be back at the plaza and somebody had played a trick on her!

But now there were so many shouting voices that she grew a little fearful. Surely six children could not make that much noise!

The next thing she knew, the top of the carton was ripped off and a man's voice was saying, "Well, I'll be a horny toad!"

Holly stood up, blinking in the dazzling sun. A chorus of surprised cries greeted her. As she looked about, Holly could hardly believe her eyes. Grouped around the back of the truck was a crowd of children dressed in various costumes of bright yellow, green, red, and purple. Beside her stood the astonished driver.

"That's a nice costume," a pretty, dark-haired girl spoke up.

Holly was still a little bewildered, but she smiled. These children must be having a costume party and thought she had come to it!

"Where's the candy and soda?" called one of the older boys.

Several girls began to giggle, and one girl said to Holly, "We expected you to be candy and soda—that's why we were all waiting for the truck."

The driver snapped his fingers. "I've got it," he said. "There were two cartons the same size in the general store, and I picked up the wrong one!"

Holly stood up.

"That's right," Holly piped up. "I was playing hide-'n'-seek, and this box was my hiding place."

The truck driver promised to go right back for the candy, then said to Holly, "Come along, little girl. Your folks'll be plenty worried wondering where you are."

Just then a sweet-faced woman with smooth black hair came over to the group and put her arm around Holly. "I'm Mrs. Beltran," she said. "What's your name?"

"Holly Hollister. I'm lost from the rest of my family."

Mrs. Beltran explained that the children of Sunrise had gathered at the school playground for their summer *fiesta*.

"What's that?" Holly asked.

Before the woman could answer, the pretty, dark-haired girl said, "Mrs. Beltran, why don't we ask Holly to stay and keep the *fiesta* a surprise for her?"

"That's a good idea," said the woman, who was in charge of the children, and asked Holly if her family would like to join them.

"Oh yes," Holly replied, delighted. Then, remembering Helen and Jack Moore, she asked if they might come also. "We're all in costume," she told Mrs. Beltran.

"Then everything is fine." The woman smiled.

Holly's eyes sparkled as she asked the truck driver if he would bring her brothers and sisters and the Moores to the *fiesta*.

"Glad to," he said.

As the truck disappeared down the road, some of the girls invited Holly to join in their games and dances while waiting for the main event of the *fiesta* to start.

Holly walked from group to group. Since she did not know any of the Spanish-type dances as well as the others, she chose to play a-tisket-a-tasket.

A boy, big for his thirteen years, came up to her. He was dressed in a devil's suit and had a sullen-looking face.

"You think you're smart breaking into our *fiesta*, don't you?" he said rudely.

"Why, I didn't do it on purpose," replied Holly, taken aback. "But I'm very glad to be here anyhow."

"Well, we don't like strangers here in Sunrise!" snapped the unpleasant lad.

Holly's new friends surrounded her, and the dark-haired girl whispered, "Don't pay any attention to him."

Another, named Ramona, addressed the big boy firmly. "Stop talking like that, Willie Boot!"

Willie scowled deeply but did not answer. Then he picked up the devil's tail, which was dragging on the ground behind him, and stalked away to the other side of the playground.

"Willie is rude to everyone," Ramona told Holly. "He gets that way from riding with Mesquite."

"Is Mequite a horse?" Holly asked.

But her question went unanswered because at that moment the Hollisters' bus and the Moores' car pulled up in front of the schoolyard. Holly raced over into her mother's outstretched arms.

"We were so worried when none of us could find you," declared Mrs. Hollister, hugging her. "And we had such good news to tell you, too. We're going to visit the Vegas at their ranch!"

Willie stalked away.

"How wonderful!" Holly cried.

"And maybe you can help us solve the mystery on the mountain," Helen said. "The ranch we're going to is right next to the Vegas'."

"What mystery?" Holly asked.

"I'll show you a book later that tells about it," Helen promised.

Ricky announced that they had brought the carton of candy and soda for the truckman. He hoped they would pass it around immediately because he was hungry.

"I looked inside the box first to make sure it had candy in it," Ricky grinned.

Holly turned to see Pete and Jack lifting out a carton like the one in which she had hidden. After they had set it down, she was introduced to Mr. and Mrs. Moore. Then Holly excitedly led her family and the Moores through the crowd to where Mrs. Beltran was directing a gay Spanish circle dance. After she had introduced them, Holly added, "They brought the candy and soda."

"Fine," said Mrs. Beltran. After the carton was opened, she said to Pete and Jack, "Would you boys like to hand out the little boxes of candy—one to a child? We'll save the soda for later."

"We'll be glad to," Pete spoke up.

He and Jack lifted out all the boxes they could hold and began to distribute them.

All of a sudden Willie Boot dashed up to Ricky, snatched his box from him, and then approached Pete.

"Give me another one," he demanded loudly.

"Sorry. Only one to a customer," Pete replied.

"Oh yeah—who says so?" Willie retorted. "And who do you think you are, strangers coming in here and telling us what to do!"

"Mrs. Beltran told us to," declared Pete firmly.

Pete tumbled to the ground.

"You mean that lady there?" Willie asked, pointing. When Pete turned to look, Willie grabbed another box from his hands and shoved him as he ran off. Pete tumbled to the ground, and the rest of the candy flew in all directions.

Mrs. Beltran saw what had happened and in a stern voice called out, "Willie Boot! Come back here immediately!"

The bully paid no attention. Instead, he tried to worm his way through the throng of children. He might have succeeded in getting away if Holly had not stepped full force on his trailing devil's tail. Willie was brought to a complete halt and, as the children shouted indignantly at him, Mrs. Beltran walked up. She was very angry.

"Give me that candy," she ordered. "You don't deserve to have any." Willie dared not disobey further and he handed over the two boxes. "And now," Mrs. Beltran said, "you'll help Pete pick up the candy you made him drop."

Willie started to grumble, but stopped as the woman looked at him severely. Grudgingly he assisted in recovering the spilled candy.

By this time Jack had finished giving out the boxes to the children and Willie's rude actions were forgotten.

Suddenly Mrs. Beltran announced, "The big *fiesta* surprise will appear very soon now. Everyone please stand at the front of the playground and watch carefully."

What a gay, noisy rush there was to reach the spot! The four older Hollister children, with Helen and Jack Moore, dashed ahead and found good places.

At the far end of the playground two men were pumping up an odd-shaped balloon. All the children watched in fascination as the balloon grew bigger and bigger and began to take on a definite shape.

"Yikes!" yelled Ricky as it slowly rose.

There was a gasp from the onlookers, then everyone burst into cheers and laughter.

Floating just above them was a giant burro, with a big man riding on its back!

The burro had long ears, and the rider wore a big red-and-yellow sombrero.

"Look at the balloon rider's nose!" Ricky howled gleefully. "It's just like a squash with a crooked neck!"

"His name is Pedro," Ramona explained through her giggles, and the local children started to shout merrily, "Hurray for old Pedro!"

Floating above them was a giant burro.

The Hollisters and the Moores learned that Pedro and his burro had been displayed this way for many years at the annual Children's Fiesta. And although everybody laughed at his funny appearance, the people of Sunrise were very fond of Pedro.

"He's sort of a reminder of the Spanish people who first settled here many, many years ago," Ramona told the guests.

To the visitors' amazement they saw that many long strings dangled from the sides of the balloon. The Sunrise boys and girls surged forward, each grabbing one of the strings.

"Come on!" Ramona cried to her new friends. "This is Pedro's parade!"

The four older Hollister children, followed by Jack and Helen Moore, dashed after Ramona, and each quickly grasped a string.

Around and around the playground went the marchers, tugging on the strings so that Pedro and the burro bounced up and down. The children sang loudly:

"Burro, burro, lead the way,
This is our *fiesta* day.
We'll have fun from morn till night,
Before you vanish like a kite."

Sue, perched on her father's shoulders, squealed in delight and her parents chuckled.

"Looks as though Pedro's going for a real ride," Mr. Hollister observed.

Mrs. Beltran nodded. "They parade all the way to town," she said.

Pete had just turned to wave at his parents when suddenly there came a whizzing noise. Everyone glanced up. An arrow had pierced Pedro's shoulder!

Hiss–ssss!

"Oh," wailed Holly, "Pedro's shrinking!"

Sure enough, the gas was leaking out of the balloon, and in a moment Pedro's head flopped to one side. By now the happy shouts of the children had turned to cries of alarm.

Pedro and the burro grew thinner and thinner, lurching this way and that. Down the balloon came, hovering lower and lower over the children's heads.

"Run, everybody!" Mrs. Beltran ordered. "The balloon's very heavy. It'll hurt you!"

CHAPTER 3

Mesquite Mike

SCRAMBLING in all directions, the children tried to get away from the fast-falling figure. But in their haste, those in the center were bumped and knocked down.

Ramona, Holly's new friend, fell to the ground so hard she lay there breathless and could not get up. Pedro and the burro, heaving and swaying, sank directly toward her! In another moment she would be covered up and injured by the tremendous balloon!

Thinking fast, Pete ran back and pulled on one of the cords with all his might. When the boy could not get it away, he yelled, "Rick! Jack! Help me pull this away!"

The three boys tugged on the strings until their arms ached. They managed to inch the heavy balloon away from Ramona just in time.

The next second the huge figure collapsed with a loud *hiss-ss* and dropped rapidly to the ground. Pete and Jack stepped aside just in time, but Ricky was unable to make it. The great rubbery mass landed squarely on top of him!

"Help! Help! My brother's trapped!" Pam shouted in terror, racing toward the spot where Ricky was covered by the folds of rubber.

By this time Mr. and Mrs. Hollister and Mrs. Beltran had reached the scene and frantically tried to help pull the balloon off Ricky. Even little Sue lifted with all her strength.

"I see where he is!" Pete yelled, pointing to something moving under the burro's head. "And look!"

Suddenly out of a hole in the rubber popped Ricky's head! With a grin the boy climbed nimbly through, a penknife in his hand.

"It didn't hurt me too much," he said. "Gee, I'm sorry I had to spoil Pedro to get out."

"Never mind Pedro," Mrs. Beltran said in relief. "I'm glad you're all right. The *fiesta* balloon can be repaired." Then she looked around the playground and added, "Whoever was mean enough to shoot the arrow into Pedro should be punished."

"Oh, see up there!" Pam cried. "Someone's peeking over the edge of the school roof."

At once all eyes turned in the direction of the one-story building. A boy's head ducked down out of sight.

"Come on, let's get him!" Pete shouted, racing forward. "I'll bet he's the one who shot the arrow—right from the roof."

The next second the other children took up the chase and followed Pete pell-mell across the playground.

"The rider's going to catch Willie!"

"How'll we get up there?" Jack asked one of the local boys.

"From inside. I'll show you."

But it was not necessary to go inside. As they rounded the corner of the school to go in, the boys and girls were just in time to see a boy run out of the door.

"It's Willie Boot!" Pam cried out, recognizing the devil suit.

Willie had added something else to his costume. A bow was slung over his shoulder, and in his belt were several arrows.

Mrs. Beltran came running up and ordered Willie to stop. But he did not obey her. Instead he dashed ahead as fast as he could. The children were immediately on his trail. Pete Hollister soon outdistanced the others and was slowly gaining on Willie.

"Get him, Pete!" shouted Ricky.

His brother had almost caught up to the fleeing bully when suddenly hoofbeats sounded on the dirt road in front of the school. A man on a skinny horse turned off the road and came galloping full speed toward Willie Boot. The rider was as thin as his horse and had a grizzly beard. Much of his face was shaded by a battered ten-gallon hat with a hole in the brim.

"A cowboy!" Ricky shouted.

"He's going to catch Willie for us!" cried Holly, and the boys and girls stopped running.

But in a moment everybody saw that just the opposite was going to happen. The man leaned far over, quickly lifted Willie up to the saddle in front of him, and galloped off in a cloud of dust.

"Crickets! He sure fooled us!" Pete exclaimed in disgust.

As the children stood looking after the disappearing pair, Jack Moore asked, "Who is the cowboy that rescued Willie?"

Ramona supplied the answer. "Mesquite Mike."

"Oh," Holly put in, "Mesquite isn't a horse? He's a man?"

Ramona nodded and went on to say that Willie went about a lot with Mesquite—he was a distant relative.

"The ranchers around here don't like Mesquite," she said. "They say he's shiftless and nobody knows how he makes a living—or even where he lives."

"I think he teaches Willie to act mean," remarked the pretty, dark-eyed girl, to which the other Sunrise children solemnly agreed.

When the visitors returned to the playground, Mr. Hollister called his family together and announced it was time to leave. Mr. and Mrs. Moore said they must be on their way too.

"Why don't we have lunch together?" suggested Mrs. Hollister. "I'm sure we're all hungry after so much excitement."

"That would be very nice," said Mrs. Moore. "Suppose we meet at the Plaza Hotel in Sunrise."

After thanking Mrs. Beltran and the local children for letting them share in the *fiesta* fun, the travelers said good-by and walked out to where the Hollister bus and the Moore car were parked.

As the Hollisters drove off, Sue piped up, "Let's play *fiesta* after lunch!"

The travelers said good-by.

"Don't forget," said her father, "that we're going to Mr. Vega's ranch. It's called Cottonwood Ranch."

"I forgot," said Sue.

By the time they reached the hotel, the Moores were waiting for them. The group went to the dining room, and a waiter placed two long tables together next to a side window.

The only other diners in the room were four men talking quietly in a far corner. From their trousers, cow boots, and tanned faces, the children judged they were ranchers. When the men saw the youngsters' new outfits, they smiled.

The waiter had the tables ready. "Suppose you children sit at one table and your parents at the other," he said.

"I want to sit next to you, Helen," said Holly, "and hear all about your mountain mystery."

"We all want to hear it," said Pam.

"All right," Helen agreed.

After everyone had given his order, Mrs. Moore took a red book from her large handbag and handed it to her daughter.

"This is our big secret," Helen almost whispered, glancing around the room as if she feared someone might spy on her.

"You mean that book's a secret?" Ricky inquired skeptically.

"Not exactly," Jack spoke up. "But something inside it is."

Helen explained, still in a low voice, that the red volume was a very, very old storybook about Mexico.

"This book may lead us to the cave."

"But the reason it's our special secret is—" She paused, a dreamy look in her eyes.

"Go on," begged Pam.

"Well," resumed Helen, "this book may lead Jack and me to the Cave of the Dollmakers on Mystery Mountain!"

Holly's eyes grew very large. "Oo-oh," she said. "That sounds spooky!"

"You mean," Ricky asked eagerly, "that you're going to look for a mountain where dollmakers used to live?"

"Yes," Helen replied. "We think it may be near the dude ranch we're going to visit."

"But you said the book is about Mexico," Pam remarked.

"Sure," Jack answered. "But a long time ago this part of the United States was part of old Mexico."

"You're right," said Pete. "We learned that in school last year. I never heard about the dollmakers, though."

Helen opened the book and pointed to a sketch of a tall mountain. On top of it was a very odd rock formation with a small clump of trees, one of them standing higher than the rest. The Hollisters leaned over to look closely at the picture.

"The ancient dollmakers lived in this cave and it's somewhere in Mystery Mountain," she explained. "And," she added, "people say there are still a lot of dolls in the cave."

"Oh, wouldn't it be wonderful to find them?" Pam cried enthusiastically.

"Hasn't anybody ever searched for the cave before?" Pete asked.

"Yes," Jack answered. "Many people have started to hunt for it, but they've all been scared away."

"Scared away?" echoed the Hollisters. "Why?"

Jack and his sister exchanged glances before Helen replied, "Because they say Mystery Mountain growls like a ferocious bear!"

Holly and Sue jumped a little at these startling words, but Ricky asked doubtfully, "Who ever heard of a mountain growling?"

"Well," Jack declared, "Helen and I are going to find out for ourselves if it does and maybe we'll be the very first people to discover the dollmakers' cave!"

"Yikes!" Ricky burst out. "I wish we could go exploring for Mystery Mountain with you!"

"Dad, our horn's been taped down!"

"We do too. Ask your mother and dad."

Mr. and Mrs. Hollister said that if they stayed long enough, they might go looking for the mountain at least once.

"Hurrah!" Ricky cried.

Suddenly everyone was startled to hear the horn of the Hollisters' bus go *beep, beep, beep!* This was followed by the sound of the Moores' horn tooting.

"Who's doing that?" Mr. Hollister and Mr. Moore cried, annoyed.

Now instead of an intermittent sound, both horns blew continuously.

"Maybe the cars are in someone's way," Mrs. Hollister suggested.

The two men and the children dashed out of the restaurant. The women, curious also, went to the door to look. Pete reached the bus first and called out:

"Dad, our horn's been taped down!"

He ripped a broad piece of adhesive from the steering wheel.

It was found that the Moore car had been given the same treatment.

"Just some boy's idea of a prank," Mrs. Hollister said forgivingly. "Perhaps he thought it was too quiet in Sunrise!"

They all looked up and down the street, but no one was in sight at the moment. Returning to the restaurant, the group found that their meal had been served. Everyone sat down and started to eat the delicious food.

A moment later a startled cry came from Helen Moore. "My book! It's gone!" she wailed. "Did one of you take it?"

"Why no," everyone answered.

"But somebody took it," Helen insisted. "Oh dear, if someone's stolen it, he might find Mystery Mountain before we do!"

CHAPTER 4

Lost Lambs

HELEN MOORE was so heartbroken at losing her Mexican storybook about Mystery Mountain that she could hardly hold back the tears. Jack, too, was dismayed and his parents as well.

"Maybe it only fell on the floor," Pete suggested hopefully and got down to look, but the book was not there.

"We'll ask the waiter," said Mrs. Moore. "He may have laid it away while we were eating."

But when they called the man he said that he had not seen it. Now a search began in earnest. Even the four ranchers joined in, looking on tables, chairs and serving trays. But the little red volume was nowhere in the room.

"Sure am sorry, ma'am," one of the ranchers said to Mrs. Hollister. "Things just seem to vamoose around here!"

"Did you lose a book too?" Holly asked him.

The man smiled. "No, little lady. We've been losing sheep. Just been talkin' 'bout how we're going to catch the rustler!"

"The storeman wasn't fooling after all," Pam whispered to her mother.

"I thought rustling days were over," Pete said.

The young rancher looked grim. "No indeed. We still have 'em out West here."

Then the four men excused themselves and left the restaurant.

"Did you hear that!" Ricky exclaimed. "Rustlers! Yikes, am I glad I have this cowboy outfit. Ride 'em, ranger!" And he raced around a table.

But Helen was not so happy. "Oh, dear," she wailed. "How can we find Mystery Mountain without the sketch?"

"Here comes the hotel owner," said Mr. Moore, as the man approached. "Maybe he can help us."

He asked if the man had noticed anyone leave the hotel with a red book, but the owner shook his head.

"What'll we do?" Helen asked.

"Ride 'em, ranger!"

Suddenly Pete pointed to the window alongside their table. "Look!" he cried.

Everyone saw that the screen had been torn from the frame a few inches. Pete snapped his fingers.

"That horn-blowing wasn't any joke!" he declared. "Somebody wanted to get us all out of here just long enough to reach in and grab the book off the table!"

"Good reasoning," Mr. Moore remarked. "The person must have wanted it badly to go to all that trouble."

"But who would want to steal it?" Helen asked sadly.

Mrs. Hollister suggested that whoever the guilty person was, he had been outside the window and overheard their conversation about Mystery Mountain.

The children ran to the window and peered out, but now the streets were deserted. The residents of Sunrise had all gone home to take their midday siestas.

"We'd better finish our lunch now," advised Mrs. Hollister. Smiling consolingly at Helen, she added, "We're all sorry about your book, but I have a feeling it may turn up somewhere."

Helen looked a little more cheerful at this. As the group resumed eating, Ricky had an idea. "Let's hunt for clues outdoors," he whispered to the other children. "We can eat fast and finish before the others."

Eager to do this, all the youngsters hastened through the rest of the meal. Promising their parents not to go far away, the seven children rushed from the hotel.

"It *is* Mesquite!"

"Where'll we look first?" Helen asked as they reached the sidewalk.

Everything was very quiet and no one was in sight. But before they could decide which way to go, the children heard the sound of hoofbeats.

"Maybe that's the bad man," said Ricky. "Let's find out!"

Ahead of them, at the end of the street, was a man on horseback, going along at a slow trot. The rider was very thin and the horse very scrawny. On the man's head was an old ten-gallon hat with a hole in the brim.

"Hey! He looks like Mesquite Mike!" Ricky exclaimed loudly.

Hearing the boy, the rider turned in his saddle and looked back at the children. Holly clutched Pam's arm.

"It *is* Mesquite!" she whispered.

Instantly the rider dug his spurs into the horse's sides and galloped off around the corner.

"Well," exclaimed Pete. "You'd almost think he's afraid of us!"

"Maybe he is," remarked Pam thoughtfully. "After all, he took Willie Boot away."

"Do you suppose he stole the book?" Holly asked the others.

"I'll bet he did," said Jack. "Or Willie."

"But how would they know about the book?" Helen argued. "We never told anyone."

Pete said he thought that Willie was looking for a chance to play another mean joke, this one on the Hollisters and the Moores. He had been spying on them outside the restaurant window.

"I'm going to look for footprints," he announced.

Pete ran up to the window, dropped to his knees and examined several footprints in the dirt. Some were smaller than others.

"A man's and a boy's," he surmised. "And both wearing cowboy boots."

The children discussed the suspicious pair as they went back to the front of the hotel.

"If that awful boy has my book, I'll probably never see it again," Helen sighed.

"Not at all, Sis," said Jack. "We'll find Willie and make him give it back!"

"And if we're around, we'll help you," offered Pete.

"You bet we will!" the other Hollisters shouted.

"I can't be sad long with you Hollisters," Helen smiled. "I guess that's why they call you the Happy Hollisters."

Just then the children's parents came out and the Hollisters said, "Good-by, we'll see you soon!"

They hurried into the bus and waved as Mr. Hollister drove down the street and out of town. Once more they went up and down the rolling countryside. Here and there grew clumps of chaparral and piñon bushes.

Ricky's nose was flattened against the window as he watched several cowboys herding cattle. He imagined being out there with the rangers, helping them round up the steers.

"Is something wrong?"

"I could use my lariat I got at the pueblo," he was thinking when Holly, who was up front, cried out:

"Look, Daddy! There's a little girl sitting all alone by the road up ahead!"

Mr. Hollister slowed down as they neared the child.

"Daddy, she's crying!" Sue said.

"John, we'd better investigate," Mrs. Hollister observed anxiously. "Perhaps the little girl is ill."

"Or she might be lost," Pam suggested.

Mr. Hollister stopped the bus alongside the child. Pam opened the door and jumped down.

"Is something wrong?" she asked, kneeling in front of her.

Instead of answering, the girl sobbed harder than ever. By this time the other children and their parents were out of the bus.

"Don't you feel well?" Pam asked softly.

"I—I'm all right," the child managed to say, wiping her tears. "But my—" She choked on a sob and could not go on.

Mrs. Hollister bent down and put a comforting arm about the child. Taking out a handkerchief, she patted the little girl's eyes. "If you'll tell us what the trouble is," she said kindly, "we may be able to help you."

"I—I've lost my—my *sheep!*" she burst out, her big brown eyes once more brimming with tears.

"Lost your sheep?" Sue echoed, and, putting her rosy face close to the other child's, asked very seriously, "Is your name Little Bo-Peep?"

Sue's funny question made the unhappy girl forget her sadness for a moment, and a smile lit up her pretty face. She was about eight years old, with a delicate olive skin and black curly hair.

Now she shook her head. "No, I'm not Little Bo-Peep, though I have lost some sheep. My name is Dolores—Dolores Vega."

The Hollisters were startled.

"From Cottonwood Ranch?" Pam asked excitedly.

"Yes," Dolores answered. "How do you know where I live?"

Mrs. Hollister explained that they were on their way to Cottonwood Ranch this very moment and told Dolores why. Hearing this made the little girl brighten up.

"Would you like to ride to your ranch with us?" Pam asked her.

Dolores, tired from her long search, said she would like this very much. She got in and sat between Pam and Holly. For the first time, she noticed their fur-trimmed suits and Pam explained how they happened to have them.

As the bus rolled along, the Hollister children began to ask Dolores questions about the lost sheep. She said that among them were baby lambs and she was very worried about their safety. The girl added that she liked to hug the lambs because they were so cuddly and warm. A little later Dolores leaned forward.

"Please turn right at the next road," she told Mr. Hollister. "It leads right to our ranch."

Mr. Hollister did so, and in a short time they came to a series of low buildings set in a beautiful grove of cottonwood trees.

"That's our home," Dolores smiled.

"It's beautiful," Pam told her.

"I'm glad you're coming to visit us," Dolores said.

The ranch house was built in an L shape with a lovely patio, around which were big bright flowers. Near by was the barn made of rough timbers and adobe mud. As Mr. Hollister pulled up in front of the house, a man came out of the door.

"John Hollister!" he exclaimed, running up and shaking hands most vigorously with his old friend.

"Frank Vega!"

"Frank Vega!" cried Mr. Hollister.

Mr. Vega, who was a head shorter than Mr. Hollister, had a pleasant smile. Like Dolores, he had curly black hair and a round tanned face.

"It's a long time since we last met," said Mr. Hollister, then introduced his family.

As Mr. Vega met one after the other, he noticed his daughter in the bus.

"Well," he said, "I see you've already made the acquaintance of my Dolores."

At this moment a pretty Spanish-looking woman came from the doorway, followed by a boy of Pete's age. The Vega boy was named Diego. He was broad-shouldered and strong and his white teeth glistened when he smiled.

Mrs. Vega invited the Hollisters to come in and sit down in the long combination living and dining room. It was attractively furnished with Spanish American furniture and draperies. There was an oversized fireplace in one corner of the room.

"Years ago, before you moved here, you asked me to visit you," Mr. Hollister remarked. Then he chuckled. "Now, thanks to Mrs. Vega's special cowboy outfits, my whole family has arrived."

The woman laughingly said how pleased she was, not only to see them all, but to find the Hollister children wearing the clothes she had designed. Mrs. Vega explained that she raised rabbits and used their fur to trim the costumes.

"Oh, can we please see the bunnies?" Sue begged eagerly.

"Our sheep did not stray off by themselves!"

Mrs. Vega smiled and promised they would all watch the rabbits being fed later on. Then the talk turned to more general matters and the children gathered before the fireplace.

Diego began to tell them about Cottonwood Ranch. He said that it was a hundred miles long.

"Yikes!" Ricky cried. "A hundred miles! How many days does it take you to get around the place?"

"We can do it in a few hours," Diego replied with a grin, "by using Dad's airplane."

Ricky's eyes popped with excitement and Pete whistled. "You have a plane all your own?" he asked in amazement.

Diego explained that a plane was absolutely necessary in running a ranch the size of Cottonwood.

"It's a great help now in our search for the missing sheep," he said. "Dad's been flying since early morning looking for them."

The boy added that about twenty-five sheep had not returned with the main flock after a storm a few days ago, and there had been no sign of them since.

Here Holly piped up, "It's sad that the cute little lambs are lost, too."

"We only hope they've stayed with the other sheep," Dolores said.

"Won't they all find their way back eventually?" Pam asked.

Diego replied seriously. "We're afraid not. Those sheep had no herder, and Dad suspects that they did not stray off by themselves."

The Hollisters stared at him, and Pete asked the question all of them were thinking. "Somebody took the sheep?"

As Diego nodded, Ricky bounced out of his chair. "Rustlers! Oh boy!"

Mr. Vega, who had walked over, said, "That's what it adds up to, Ricky."

"I know what!" the little boy shouted. "Let's hunt for your lost sheep right away!"

At this moment a strange voice said from the doorway, "No. That would be too dangerous."

CHAPTER 5

A Dog's New Name

A SLENDER old man limped into the Vegas' living room. He was dressed in khaki work trousers and a green shirt.

"Today is not good for children's adventures," he spoke solemnly. "Last night there was a cradle moon. That's only good for fishing—nothing else."

Dolores giggled at the astonished look on the faces of the Hollister children. Then Mr. Vega said:

"I'd like you to meet Truchas. He served my family many years as a sheepherder. But he no longer goes out on the range except to ride with Diego and Dolores."

Truchas smiled and did not seem so solemn any more. He shook hands with the Hollisters, saying he was very glad to meet them.

"Mr. Truchas, how can you tell when things are going to happen before they do?" Holly asked him in awe.

The old sheepherder seated himself on a stool in front of the fireplace and replied in his deep voice, "My grandfather taught me many secrets of telling the future. But I promised never to reveal them."

The five children from Shoreham felt a little shivery when he said this. How mysterious it sounded!

Mr. Vega laughed. "It's surprising how many of Truchas' predictions come true," he admitted.

"And it's surprising how often the moon foretells good fishing," Mrs. Vega added with a wink. "You see, truchas means 'trout' in Spanish. That's how Truchas got his nickname."

Pete and Ricky eagerly questioned the old man about fishing in the river near by. Both boys loved to fish and had lots of fun back home seeing who could hook the biggest catch.

"We'll go fishin' tomorrow," Truchas said, and shuffled off.

Soon it was time to feed the rabbits. Dolores and Diego led the way to a long row of wire pens some distance from the ranch house. The cages were filled with white rabbits, twitching their pink noses and flopping their long ears.

"They're darling!" Holly exclaimed. "May I pick one up?"

"Of course," replied Diego, lifting the lid of one pen.

Reaching down, he picked up a plump rabbit by the ears and put it in Holly's arms.

"Oh, you sweet thing!" the little girl murmured, stroking the animal's soft fur. "He isn't scared of me," Holly added in a pleased voice.

Dolores gave the other children handfuls of lettuce leaves. Instantly each child ran to one of the pens, opened the lid, and began dropping in the pieces of green vegetable.

"He isn't scared of me."

"Oh! See the bunnies hippity-hop!" Sue squealed with joy.

They all laughed as the rabbits scampered after the food, their noses twitching harder than ever, and their snowball tails bobbing.

"Your bunnies have very good manners," Pam commented. "They take only little nibbles even though they're real hungry."

Just then Holly noticed that one rabbit had no lettuce to chew. "Guess he didn't hop fast enough," she thought. "Poor thing."

Holly was about to give it a lettuce leaf when an idea popped into her mind. "Maybe the bunny will sit up and beg like our dog Zip," she told herself. "I'll try him."

Holding the leaf where the rabbit could see it, just above the open pen, Holly coaxed gently, "Now, bunny, nice bunny, sit up and ask for your supper."

The rabbit's shiny eyes gazed hungrily at the lettuce which Holly dangled above him.

"Sit up!" she urged once more, waving the green leaf back and forth.

The next instant Holly let out a startled, "Oh!"

With a great hop, the rabbit sprang out of the pen, landing right at her feet. But before she could make a move to catch him, he had scooted between her feet and ran off toward a field.

"We must catch him!" Dolores cried. "If he gets into the buffalo grass, he'll be gone for good!"

Off the children raced after the fleet-footed rabbit. As Holly ran along, she wailed:

"Oh, dear! If the bunny gets lost, it's all my fault!"

At that moment a large, smooth-haired dog with a pointed nose and a long, swishing tail appeared around the corner of the barn and joined the chase.

"Look out!" Ricky yelled. "That dog'll eat the rabbit up!"

His brother and sisters were frightened too, as they saw the big animal bound after the rabbit. But Dolores and Diego told the Hollisters not to worry.

"That's our dog Frijoles," Diego said. "He won't hurt the rabbit." Calling loudly, he cried, "Go get him, Frijoles!"

The Hollister children could hardly believe what they now saw. When Frijoles caught up to the rabbit, he circled around and headed the fleeing animal back toward the children.

"There, you see," Dolores said, as the furry runaway scampered in their direction.

When he came near Holly, she reached down and caught the rabbit. How thankful she was that he hadn't been lost!

"I'm sorry I teased the bunny," Holly said, and immediately fed him several large lettuce leaves.

The Vegas' dog trotted up to Sue and licked one of the little girl's hands in a friendly way while she patted him with the other.

"What a funny, funny name you have," Sue giggled. "Free-Free—" she started to say, but could not pronounce the rest of the dog's name.

"Can't you say Frijoles?" Dolores asked. "Pronounce it Free-ho-lees. It means *beans* in Spanish."

"Then why don't you just call him Beans?" Holly suggested. "That's a lot easier to say."

Diego grinned. "I think Holly's right," he said to Dolores. "Perhaps we should call Frijoles just plain Beans—at least while the Hollisters are visiting us."

"Then he should have a new birth certificate," Holly laughed. "Here, Beans!"

The friendly dog came over to her, wagging his tail so hard that he stirred up a little puff of dust on the ground.

"Well, you girls rename Frijoles then," Diego chuckled. "I'm going to show Pete and Ricky Dad's plane."

"Frijoles! What a funny name for a dog!"

As the boys left, the girls hurried into the ranch house, where Dolores took a pen and some paper from her mother's writing desk. Handing them to Pam, she said:

"Will you write out a new birth certificate for Frijoles?"

The girls giggled as Pam sat down at the desk. She picked up the pen, then asked:

"When was Frijoles born?"

"Three years ago," Dolores replied.

Pam wrote down a few lines on the paper. Then she arose and made her expression very serious as she called Frijoles over. The four girls stood solemnly around the dog, who looked up questioningly at Pam. She placed her hand on his head.

"We will now have the naming ceremony," she announced. "We hereby declare your new name to be Beans!"

Then, holding up the paper, Pam read:

Beans Vega

born August three years ago

Dr. Hollister

The others shouted with laughter as Pam put the certificate between the dog's teeth. The ceremony was over.

"Beans, do you like your new name?" Sue asked anxiously.

The dog tossed his head, dropped the paper and barked, *arf, arf.*

"He's saying okay," Dolores laughed, as Beans picked up the paper again.

Meanwhile, the boys had walked to the big barn where Mr. Vega kept his airplane. As the door swung shut behind them, Ricky and Pete gasped in amazement upon seeing a beautiful, red, six-passenger plane.

"Yikes!" Ricky exclaimed. "I wish we had one like this in Shoreham."

"So do I," Pete agreed eagerly. "Only one with pontoons, so we could land on the lake."

Diego and his friends climbed into the cabin of the plane and he showed them the instrument panel.

A plane in the barn!

"Be careful never to touch this button," Diego warned them, "because it starts the motor."

After they had looked through the well-equipped ship for a while, Diego and Pete climbed out, but Ricky remained in the cabin.

"This has a nifty rudder," Pete remarked, looking up as the two walked around to the back of the plane.

Diego showed Pete the tail assembly and explained how the wires controlled the rudder.

"Is the airplane heavy?" Pete asked.

"Yes," replied Diego, "but you wouldn't think so. It's very easy to lift the tail. Let's try it."

He and Pete put their hands in back of the plane and pushed, tilting the plane up.

"See?" Diego said.

"You'd never believe it," Pete remarked. "It sure is a swell job."

Inside the plane, however, the sudden movement had caused Ricky to lose his balance near the instrument panel. He fell directly against the starter button!

With a deafening roar, the motor sprang to life and the propeller began to spin.

To Ricky's horror, the plane started moving slowly toward the closed barn door!

CHAPTER 6

Pete's Narrow Escape

As THE plane started rolling forward, Pete and Diego cried out in alarm.

"Help me hang on to it, Pete!" Diego shouted, as the plane inched closer and closer to the barn door.

The boys tried to hold it back with all their might, but could not stop it. Suddenly Pete saw a cowboy's rope coiled over a post. Quickly grabbing the rope, Pete lassoed one end to the tail of the plane and tied the other to the post.

Pete lassoed the tail of the plane.

It worked! The plane was held firmly with the propeller just inches from the barn door. Diego ran around to the cabin and jumped in to turn off the motor.

"Wow!" exclaimed Ricky, pale with fear. "Thanks, fellows. I thought I was going to take off right through the barn door!"

As he said this, both boys' fathers burst into the barn looking very worried.

"Did someone start the plane motor?" Mr. Vega asked quickly.

Diego told how the accident had happened, and Ricky said:

"I—I sure learned a lesson. I'll never go near the instrument panel again unless someone big is with me."

Now Mr. Vega smiled and asked, "Would you boys like to see our ranch from the air sometime soon?"

"Crickets!" Pete cried. "You mean take a ride in your plane?"

As Mr. Vega nodded, Ricky shouted, *"Yippee!"* and Pete said, "That will be neat. Thank you."

After supper Dolores ran ahead of the others into the living room. "Now we'll have some Spanish music," she announced gaily. "We play and sing every night." The girl opened a cupboard alongside the fireplace.

"Why, it's full of musical instruments!" Pam exclaimed. "Do you each play one?"

"Yes," Diego replied. "We're the Vega quartet."

The visitors watched in delight as he handed a concertina to Dolores, a marimba to his father, and maracas to Mrs. Vega. Then the boy lifted down his own instrument—a beautiful shiny guitar.

"That's super!" Ricky whispered to Pete when he saw the guitar.

As the Hollisters found places on the sofa and chairs, Mr. Vega nodded to his family and they began to play the lively Spanish tune "Valencia."

Dolores' fingers flew nimbly over the concertina. Diego strummed his guitar, while Mr. Vega struck the tinkling bell tones of the marimba. All the time Mrs. Vega kept the beat with her flashing maracas.

"It's almost as good as being in Spain," Mrs. Hollister said dreamily as she listened to the lilting music.

The players switched to a different piece, which Diego said was "Jarabe Tapatio," a catchy Mexican hat dance. Presently Dolores laid down her instrument and took a large, fancy trimmed sombrero and a pair of castanets from the wall. She attached the castanets to her hands. Then, laying the hat on the floor, she began to dance around it, clicking the castanets in time to the music. As the piece neared an end, she stepped close to the brim of the hat and daintily tripped around it. As the dance finished, the Hollisters clapped loudly.

"That was beautiful," Pam declared. "Please show me how to do it while I'm here."

Dolores smiled, promising to do this. Then the singing began, first Spanish, then American. The Hollisters joined in the American songs.

She tripped around the brim of the hat.

"My, I haven't sung so much since our glee club days in college," Mr. Hollister said, grinning at Mr. Vega when the evening finished.

"Wasn't it all fun!" Pam said, tumbling weary but happy into bed. She and Holly were sharing the same room.

The following morning the children were up early and dressed in jeans and shirts. Truchas arrived to take the boys fishing. As they were getting rods and reels, Sue watched them, fascinated. Finally she looked at the elderly man and said:

"Mr. Truchas, will you please bring back some truchas so we can have truchas for supper?"

They all laughed, and Dolores said that her little friend was learning Spanish quickly.

"I'll teach you some more words if you like," she offered.

Pete, Ricky, and Diego followed Truchas to the barn, at the end of which were several stalls. The old herder went inside and brought out three horses. He introduced them as Spot, Pal, and Cutie. Then he swung Ricky up on Cutie's back, and mounted behind the boy. Diego nimbly jumped on Spot and Pete climbed onto Pal.

"I forgot my special fish pole," Truchas announced. "We'll stop for it."

They went across a little plank bridge over a gorge some distance beyond the barn. Diego explained that this was an *arroyo*. During a flash flood the rain ran off through it.

The riders cut across the range and presently came to a low adobe building with green, red, and yellow painted gourds hanging over the doorway. When Ricky asked what these were for, Truchas explained that they brought good luck.

"I hope we have some when we're fishing," Pete said, as the elderly man dismounted and went into the house.

He came out in a few minutes with a short, gnarled pole, mounted once more, and they all set off toward the river. Half an hour later as the horses picked their way through a thicket of juniper trees, they suddenly heard the gurgling of water.

In a few minutes they reached the edge of the bank and looked down into the swirling stream. It flowed through a deep cut.

Picketing their horses some distance back, Truchas and the boys baited their lines and cast them into the stream. Almost immediately Pete and Diego had strikes. Beautiful speckled trout took the hooks and leaped above the surface of the water.

"What did I tell you?" Truchas crowed. "Cradle moon *is* good for fishing!"

"You're right, Truchas!" Pete cried excitedly as he reeled in the fattest trout he had ever caught.

No sooner had he taken the fish from his hook than Ricky shouted, "I've got a big one too." After they had put the trout in a basket, he added, "Truchas hasn't caught a fish yet. Let's leave him awhile and walk down the bank a way."

"Okay," said Diego.

"Boy, that water looks cold," Pete said, as he hunted for another likely place to throw in his line.

Pete and Diego had strikes.

"It is," Diego assured him. "This river starts way up in the mountains of Colorado and the water comes from melting snow."

Pete walked on farther than the others. Soon he came to a narrow ledge which jutted out over the river.

"This is swell!" he thought. "I can throw my line clear to the center of the stream."

As he did this, he heard Diego shout, "Get back, Pete! That's a dangerous overhang!"

But before Pete could retrace his steps, he felt the earth giving way beneath his feet and he slid helplessly into the icy water.

When Pete's head bobbed to the surface in the churning stream, the boy could scarcely catch his breath he was so cold. However, he struck out for shore, swimming as fast as he could.

But every time his feet touched the gravelly shore, the swirling water carried him out into the river again.

"I'll save him with my horse!" Diego called to Ricky. "You go back to Truchas."

Ricky obeyed but he watched his brother fearfully. Oh why was Diego so slow?

Actually Diego was not gone long. He soon dashed up on Spot and rode to the water's edge some distance downstream. By this time Pete was splashing and floundering helplessly in the rapidly running stream. Ricky was fearful that his brother would be swept under.

Diego dismounted and led Spot into the river. Suddenly he slapped the horse, crying out: "Get him, Spot! Get Pete!"

Pete reached up and grabbed the saddle.

As Truchas and Ricky watched, the faithful horse swam toward the middle of the stream. Thankfully Pete reached up and grabbed the saddle.

"Come back, Spot!" Diego shouted.

The horse turned in midstream and swam to the shore, with Pete hanging to the saddle and floating on the surface of the stream.

Reaching the bank, Pete flopped on the ground to regain his breath. Truchas was waiting there with Ricky.

"I told you," the old man said, "that the cradle moon is no good for children's adventures. Only good for fishing!"

"I guess you're right," Pete agreed ruefully, as he pulled off his shirt and trousers to dry them in the sun. "I won't go on any more adventures today. I'll just concentrate on my fishing."

The little group ate a lunch they had brought, then began to tell stories. Pete asked if Diego and Truchas had ever heard of a mysterious mountain in the vicinity where there was a cave used by ancient dollmakers. The two looked at him in amazement, then burst out laughing.

"Is this a joke?" Diego asked.

"It sure isn't," Ricky burst out. "And we're going to help some friends of ours find it while we're here."

After more fishing, during which they caught the limit the law allowed, Truchas and the boys mounted their horses and started back for the ranch house.

"If you boys go ridin' alone sometime," Truchas said, "beware of the giant monster that lives in one of the mountains."

Pete and Ricky looked at each other in surprise. "The giant monster?" Pete asked. "Which mountain does he live in?"

Truchas pointed off to a distant peak. "I think it's over there somewhere."

The Hollister boys shot a glance at Diego, who to their surprise seemed to be taking Truchas' warning very much to heart.

"Diego, is there really a giant monster?"

"Yes," he murmured.

"Then tell us something about him," Pete urged.

As Diego kept still, Truchas told them that the monster lived in a cave and made a fearful noise.

"Beware of the mountain's monster!"

Pete's eyes grew wide when he heard this. "I'll bet it's the same mystery mountain I was telling you about!" he exclaimed.

"Never heard it called that," Truchas said.

"Tell me," Pete said, "does this monster growl like a bear?"

Truchas shrugged, then said, "Don't go near the monster's mountain. I wouldn't want any harm to come to you."

When Ricky and Pete asked a few more questions, Diego remained strangely silent, and the boys could tell from the expression on his face that they should not press him further.

Ricky turned toward Pete and whispered, "Another mystery! Let's go look for the monster someday."

Pete frowned at his brother and said he'd better not talk about the monster for a while. Ricky kept still but decided he was going to find out more from Diego later.

The horses trotted along in single file with Truchas in the lead. Suddenly the old man reined in his horse sharply and raised his right hand.

The boys stopped as he swung down from his saddle and crouched on the ground to examine some freshly made animal tracks. The boys dismounted also and followed his gaze.

"Sheep tracks!" Truchas announced.

Suddenly the old man spoke to Diego rapidly in Spanish.

"What did he say?" Ricky wanted to know.

"Sheep tracks!" exclaimed Truchas.

"Whenever Truchas gets excited, he always speaks in Spanish," Diego replied. "He thinks these tracks were made by my father's lost sheep!"

CHAPTER 7

Seven Little Donkeys

"COME on, let's follow the sheep tracks!" Diego urged, vaulting into the saddle.

Truchas, Ricky, and Pete mounted too and set off in the direction where the marks led. After they had ridden a couple of miles, Diego remarked, "These sheep weren't just wandering. They were driven."

"How can you tell?" Ricky asked.

"Because they went in nearly a straight line," Diego replied.

"He's right," Truchas agreed. "I saw a horse's hoof-prints. Somebody was guiding the sheep."

After the little group had traveled for another hour, Truchas halted. "We won't dare follow the tracks any farther. Darkness will come on before we get back."

"Can we pick up the trail tomorrow?" Pete asked eagerly.

When Truchas agreed to this, Ricky stood up in the stirrups and yelled, "Yi, yi!"

The sun was a big red ball setting over the distant mountains when the riders reached home. Truchas went to his cabin. The boys put their horses away, then hurried to the ranch house.

Diego burst into the living room. "Where's Dad?" he asked his mother excitedly.

Mrs. Vega said his father had gone to California on business and would not return until the next afternoon. Disappointed, the boy related to his mother and Mr. and Mrs. Hollister how they had come across the tracks of the lost sheep.

"Your father should know about this right away," Mr. Hollister said. "Can we telephone him?"

"Yes. I'll get the number," Mrs. Vega said.

The operator located Mr. Vega at his hotel. He was amazed at the news and said he would return home as quickly as possible. But it would not be until the next day.

Mrs. Vega had just hung up the telephone when everyone jumped. A vivid flash of lightning, followed by a loud thunderclap, had startled them all.

"Oh, oh," Diego said, as he looked out the window at the blackening sky. "We're going to get a honey of a storm."

"The ranch can use some water," said Mrs. Vega. "But I do hope it will not be a pounding rain. Gentle rain is good for the grass, but when it comes down in torrents, the water runs off too quickly instead of soaking into the ground."

As the sky grew darker and darker, the girls watched it eagerly. Mrs. Vega prepared a late supper. As they ate, a high wind swept over the ranch and the rain started to fall in sheets. Lightning zigzagged sharply and the thunder boomed like giant cannon.

Ricky declared he had never heard such a noise. "Maybe that mountain monster is growling too," he said.

"What monster?" the Hollister girls chorused as Dolores looked at her brother with fright in her eyes.

Ricky told them what Truchas had said. Then, before they could comment, Dolores begged that they not talk about it any more. To change the subject, Mrs. Hollister remarked:

"I've never seen a storm as severe as this one. Do you have them often?"

Mrs. Vega replied that this was a typical storm for the area. "They don't last long," she said. "But there's a tremendous amount of water. We call this a flash flood."

A high wind swept over the ranch.

"It looks like a whole river pouring down on us," Holly remarked. "Where does it go?"

"Into the *arroyo*. We'll show you when the rain stops."

As Mrs. Vega had said, the storm ceased after a few minutes and the sky cleared. Outside they could hear the rushing of water as it rolled over the surface of the arid land.

"Come on!" Diego cried presently, beckoning the children to follow him out the door.

Taking off their shoes and socks, all of them hurried from the house. They sloshed through the soggy ground to the gorge, which was twenty feet deep and led toward the river. That afternoon it had been dry. Now it was nearly filled with a churning mass of water.

"Don't go too near the edge," Diego warned the others, and added, "We'd have a hard time rescuing anyone."

Dolores told the girls that the *arroyo* had been cut by the water of many, many storms.

"It gets wider and deeper every year," she explained.

"The bridge is gone!" Ricky exclaimed suddenly. "The one we went over. How'll we get to the other side when we go after the sheep tomorrow?"

Dolores laughed. "We have to put down new planks for a bridge after every storm," she explained.

The children watched until it grew too dark to see. Then they returned to the ranch house, where the evening musical took place until bedtime.

The next morning Pete and Ricky rose early. "I want to go out and see if any water's left in the *arroyo*," Ricky said, as he put on his moccasins.

"Okay. I'll go with you."

The two boys hurried outside. When they got to the bank of the *arroyo*, they found Diego already there, gazing at the narrow stream of water that gurgled along the bottom of it.

Pete, glancing down the opposite bank, called out, "Hey! There's a ten-gallon hat. Does it belong to someone on this ranch?"

"We'll soon find out," Diego replied.

He went back to the barn and returned in a few minutes with a long pole. The boys ran along the bank

Pete stretched out as far as he could.

of the *arroyo* until they came to the hat. By this time it had tumbled into the water and was being carried along.

"Can you reach it?" Pete asked, as his friend Diego tried several times to snag the moving hat without success.

"Here, let me try," Pete said.

He took the pole in his two hands and leaned forward, with Diego holding him firmly by the waist. Ricky in turn clung to Diego's belt.

Pete stretched as far as he could and finally caught the hat. Lifting it up to the bank, he remarked:

"That sure looks beat up."

"Yes," said Diego, "and I don't think it belongs to anyone at Cottonwood." He examined the hatband. "No initials," he said, "and everyone on this ranch has his marked."

"Say," Pete exclaimed, "this hat looks just like the one Mesquite Mike was wearing in town."

"It sure does," Ricky agreed. "It had a hole in the brim just like this one. Do you suppose—"

Pete's eyes widened. "If it's Mesquite Mike's, that would prove he's been on your property!"

"And why would that hombre come here except to rustle sheep?" Diego asked excitedly. "I'm going to tell Dad to notify the state police!"

The boys took the dripping hat back to the ranch house. When Mrs. Vega saw it, she agreed that the police should be told but said Diego should wait until his father returned.

At this moment Dolores came running in from outdoors. Excitedly she asked everyone to come to the sheep barn. As they all hurried along behind her, Dolores opened the barn door and walked ahead quietly, motioning for the others to be silent. In a moment she pointed to the inside of a small pen. In one corner lay an ewe with a tiny lamb cuddled alongside her.

"Oh, isn't the baby darling?" Holly whispered. "How old is it?"

"The lamb was born last night," Dolores answered. "Mother," she added, "one of its legs is twisted. The lamb can't stand up."

The girl went over and picked up the tiny animal. One hind leg was definitely out of shape.

"What'll you do?" Pam asked sympathetically.

"I'm sure," Mrs. Vega replied, "that Truchas can fix the lamb's leg. Diego, ride over and get him."

Her son lost no time in going on the errand. When breakfast was over the children discovered that the old herdsman had manipulated the lamb's leg into place and put a splint on it as well as a veterinarian could have done. Truchas declared that the animal would be gamboling with the other lambs within a week.

"You mean she'll go with the herd?" Pam asked.

"Yes," the man said. "We usually leave the new lambs with their mothers only for a day or two. After that the mothers can recognize their own babies anywhere in the big herd."

"That's a good trick." Holly laughed.

As the Hollister children started to leave the barn, Diego told them to follow him. In another part of the barn were seven little stalls. And in them stood seven little burros!

"Oh, how cute!" Holly cried out.

"So many all alike!" Sue chimed in. "And they're such tiny horses. Are they just babies?"

"Oh no, they're full grown," Diego told her.

He explained that these were not horses, but a small breed of donkey which they used as pack animals to travel with the sheepherders and carry supplies.

"Can they carry heavy loads?" Pam wanted to know. "They seem so small."

"Burros are very strong," Diego said. "And sure-footed, too. They can climb over the narrowest mountain passes with heavy loads on their backs."

"What'll you do with the lamb?"

"What are these burros' names?" Holly asked.

"We've named them for the seven days of the week," the boy answered. "Lunes, Martes, Miércoles, Jueves, Viernes, Sábado, and Domingo."

"How funny!" Ricky chuckled. Then he added, "How can you ever remember those names?"

"It's easy," Diego said. "Just as you would say, Monday, Tuesday, Wednesday, Thursday, Friday, Saturday, and Sunday."

Dolores looked up teasingly at Pam with her big brown eyes and said, "Please don't try to change the names of our burros, will you?"

Pam laughed. "No. Beans was enough. But you won't mind if we call the burros by their American names?"

"No."

Holly stroked the nose of Domingo and remarked, "I want to ride Sunday on Monday if I can't have Tuesday on Wednesday."

The other children giggled. Then Pete said, "May we ride them?"

"Sure, we'll have a burro parade," Diego suggested. "There's one burro apiece for the Hollisters. Help me lead them out of the barn."

When the burros were standing in the barnyard, all the Hollisters except Sue swung themselves onto their backs. Dolores lifted Sue astride Sábado.

"Come on, Saturday," the little girl said. "But be careful of me."

Dolores lifted Sue astride Sabado.

Excited, the children rode back and forth on the burros.

"Isn't this wonderful?" Pam called out. "Can we take a long ride on them someday?"

Just then Sue called, "Help! Catch me!"

Before anyone could rush to her aid, Sue slipped off Sábado's back and landed face down in the dust. Diego rushed over to pick her up. Sue was crying and holding her nose.

"It hurts," she cried. "My nose is broke!"

"If it is," said Ricky, "we'll have to put a splint on it like the baby lamb's."

Everybody dismounted. By this time Mrs. Hollister, who had hurried over, examined Sue's nose. She found that it was not broken, and had only a little scratch on it.

"I'll get my nurse's kit," Dolores offered, and dashed off toward the ranch house.

She returned a few minutes later carrying a little blue box with a red cross on it. Then she opened the kit and expertly put a small adhesive bandage on Sue's nose. The children put the burros away, and as they returned to the ranch house, they heard the telephone ringing.

"Maybe it's Dad!" Diego said, running to answer it.

But the call was not from Mr. Vega. Turning, the boy said:

"Pete, it's for you."

CHAPTER 8

Young Pilots

"TELEPHONE for me?" Pete asked in surprise. "Who is it?"

"He didn't say."

Pete picked up the phone. "Hello. This is Pete Hollister."

"Hi, Pete! This is Jack Moore. I'm having a swell time. How about you?"

"Nifty. Have you been to Mystery Mountain yet?"

"Same here. And we suspect Mesquite Mike."

"No," Jack answered soberly. "Nobody here has ever heard of it. And we haven't found the book that was stolen, so we don't know where to look."

"That's too bad," said Pete. "Maybe something will turn up."

"Oh, we have plenty to do," Jack told him. "A lot of sheep are missing from Bishop's Ranch and we've been out looking for them."

Pete whistled. "Honestly? That's just what's happened at Cottonwood. We think we're on the trail of them, though."

"Maybe ours are in the same place. Mr. Bishop thinks they were rustled."

"Same here. And we suspect Mesquite Mike," said Pete. "Have you found out where he lives?"

"No. But listen to this: Helen and I got a note from Willie Boot."

"What!" Pete exclaimed.

"Yes. He said he didn't want us to go home thinking he was the one who had ruined Pedro the donkey at the *fiesta*. It was somebody else."

"I don't believe it!" Pete exclaimed.

"Neither do we. But Willie said somebody else on the school roof was responsible," Jack went on. "He wouldn't tell on him, he said."

Pete wanted to give Willie Boot the benefit of the doubt but he found it hard to swallow the story and said so.

"Well, let's forget him," said Jack. "Say, Pete, how about your coming over here sometime?"

"It's Dad!" Diego cried.

"Sure. I'll ask my folks and give you a call."

"And bring Pam. Helen says to say hello. Well, I have to go now. So long. Be seeing you."

"You bet. Good-by."

Pete told the others what he had learned and all of them were puzzled about Willie Boot. While they were discussing him, the group heard a car approaching.

"It's Dad!" Dolores cried, and ran out to meet him.

Diego followed, and their father had hardly stopped before the boy was telling about the sheep tracks and the clue of the hat that seemed to point to Mesquite Mike as the rustler.

"Don't you think you ought to notify the police?" Diego asked.

"I will," Mr. Vega replied. "It's a fine suggestion. All the ranchers have felt for a long time that Mesquite

Mike wasn't honest but we had no idea he had taken to rustling."

Mr. Vega went at once to the telephone and reported his son's suspicions. Then, returning to his family and the Hollisters, he said:

"I believe I'll do a little sleuthing in my plane after lunch. Anybody want to go?"

There was a chorus of "Oh yes!" from the children.

Mrs. Hollister laughed. "I'm sure there's not room for all of you in the plane. We'd better let Mr. Vega choose his passengers."

The ranch owner smiled. "It'll be a tight squeeze but I believe I can fit all seven of them in," he told her.

"Goody!" shouted Sue, who had been fearful she would be left out.

After lunch everyone went outside to see the searchers take off in Mr. Vega's plane. Pam was sorry there was not room for her father to go along. Walking up to him, she put a hand on his arm.

"Dad," she said, "wouldn't you like to ride in my place?"

"That's nice of you, my dear," he said, touched by her generosity, "but you join the others. I don't mind staying here."

Pam was not going to give up so easily. "You like to ride horseback," she said. "Wouldn't you and Truchas like to search on the ground?"

"Fine idea," Mr. Hollister laughed. "It'll do me good to get some exercise."

"When do we start?" Ricky asked impatiently.

"Right away if you're ready," was the reply.

The children raced to the barn. Opening the big door, they pushed the airplane out and wheeled it into a nearby field which Mr. Vega used for his runway.

The children climbed into the plane. Mr. Vega entered last and closed the door. He sat in the pilot's seat and started the engine. His passengers' eager faces peered out of the windows and they waved good-by. The ship taxied down the homemade runway, then headed about into the wind.

"Here we go!" Mr. Vega said as he gave it the throttle.

The engine roared as the craft sped across the field, then rose gently into the air.

Diego sat in a chair alongside his father. The others took places back of them with Sue on Pam's lap and Holly on Dolores's. Pete and Ricky occupied the rear seats.

As the plane circled over the ranch Mr. Vega asked the boys to guide him to the spot where they had seen the sheep tracks.

"It was not far from the river," Diego told him.

As the ship sped toward the spot, the boy reached into a compartment alongside the seat and pulled out a pair of powerful binoculars.

"There, I think we're over the place now," he said.

Mr. Vega swooped lower, while his son scanned the ground with his glasses. He could see no sign of the sheep tracks.

"Are you sure this is the spot?" Mr. Vega asked, as he banked the plane and headed over the territory again.

"Yes, this is right," Pete spoke up. "I remember that formation of juniper trees."

"But there are no tracks down there now," Diego insisted.

"Do you suppose," said Pam, "that the storm last night washed away the tracks?"

"Pam, you're a good sleuth," said Mr. Vega. "Your guess is perfect. We'll have to give up hunting for the tracks. Well, I'll show you Hollisters our ranch."

What a thrilling sight it was to look down over the vast countryside! The piñon bushes looked like tiny little blobs of green against the sandy soil. And though

The plane rose gently in the air.

the plane was high now, the mountains in the distance loomed still higher.

"I'll give you all a look at one of our herds," Mr. Vega said.

The children kept their eyes glued to the ground, but in a few minutes Pete turned to look toward Mr. Vega. He gave a whistle of surprise and all the others gazed ahead.

Diego was in the pilot's seat, his hands firmly holding the wheel!

"Crickets!" Pete exclaimed. "I didn't know you could pilot a plane, Diego!"

Diego kept his eyes straight ahead and replied without turning his head. "Sure. Dad taught me how to fly this plane, and when I'm old enough I'm going to get a pilot's license."

Mr. Vega explained that children were allowed to fly airplanes over uninhabited territory as long as an experienced pilot was with them.

"Gee, could I have a turn?" Ricky proposed.

"If you're very careful and do as I say," Mr. Vega answered. "But first, we'll let Diego keep the wheel for five minutes."

The boy flew the plane like a veteran. When the time was up, his father said:

"All right, Diego. We'll let the Hollisters have their turns now. Who'll be first?"

"Can Pam try?" Pete asked.

"Sure enough. Come on up here, Pam."

"This isn't a bronc," the pilot said.

The girl rose and made her way to the front of the plane. Mr. Vega steadied the wheel as she seated herself.

"Keep the nose level with the horizon," he instructed her. "Don't hold on to the wheel as if it were a bucking bronc."

Pam was a bit fearful but she tried to do exactly as Mr. Vega had told her. The plane, however, did not fly as it had for Diego. First the nose went down a little and Pam pulled back on the wheel. Then the nose rose again but too sharply.

"Hey, Pam! You're giving us a roller-coaster ride!" Ricky shouted.

"This is fun," Holly declared gleefully. "But be sure you don't take us up to the moon, Pam."

This made her sister giggle so hard that the wheel jiggled and the plane wobbled a bit. Mr. Vega took it, saying:

"You did very well for your first try, Pam. I think you will make a very good girl pilot. Ricky, how about you?"

The red-haired boy scrambled up to the pilot's seat, but he could not hold the plane completely level either. Although it did not go up and down so sharply as it had for Pam, it felt like a children's roller coaster.

"Okay, Holly. You're next," Mr. Vega said, smiling at the pig-tailed girl.

Holly did as well as her brother. Then it was Pete's turn. The boy had observed Diego very carefully and tried to imitate him.

"You're doing swell!" Diego said admiringly as Pete guided the plane smoothly.

After he had been at the controls for about three minutes, Mr. Vega reached back for Sue. Lifting her forward, he took the pilot's seat and held the little girl on his lap.

"Now, put your hands on the wheel," he told her.

Sue did this, but bounced up and down in the seat as if she were on horseback and all the children laughed. Just as Sue's turn was over, Dolores said:

"Look up ahead. That's one of our flocks."

On the slope of a hillside could be seen a good-sized patch of white.

"How many sheep are in that flock?" Pete asked.

"About a thousand."

"And one herder takes care of all of them?"

"A herder and a cook," Diego replied, "and they have five burros to carry their supplies."

Mr. Vega banked the plane and flew low over the flock. Two men standing near them waved their hats and the children waved back.

"Why do you raise your sheep so far from your home?" Pam asked.

Mr. Vega explained that there was not water enough for good pasture closer to the ranch house. The flocks had to be taken far down the range and up on the hillside where the vegetation was lush in the summer.

As they flew back, Pete asked if he might use the glasses. A mountain they were passing suddenly looked

Mr. Vega flew low over the flock.

to him like the sketch of Mystery Mountain in Helen and Jack Moore's old book! Could this be it? He asked Mr. Vega what the name of the mountain was.

"Around here we call it Serpent Peak, but I guess it has had many names over a period of years."

About halfway back to the ranch house Holly took the binoculars and scanned the ground below them. All at once she cried out:

"Look! I see something moving down there! Maybe it's the lost sheep!"

Mr. Vega circled the plane. Something *was* moving about in a piñon thicket. He found a strip of open ground and brought the plane down in a long glide.

But as the wheels touched the earth suddenly a frightened dogie dashed from the piñon thicket and ran directly in front of the plane.

"Look out!" the children screamed.

Mr. Vega swerved the plane sharply. He missed the young calf, who scampered off, but his craft skidded directly toward the edge of a deep *arroyo*.

"We're going to crash into it!" Pam shrieked.

CHAPTER 9

Missing Children

WOULD the plane stop in time? Mr. Vega was trying desperately to bring it to a halt short of the *arroyo*.

The children held their breath and clutched one another. The plane slowed down at the lip of the deep gully, but the right front wheel slid over the edge. The plane teetered precariously for a few seconds, then stood still.

"Thank goodness," Mr. Vega whispered prayerfully. Aloud he said, "Don't move, any of you, until I give the word. Any sudden movement may tip us over. Diego, crawl out the emergency door in the rear and hang on to the tail. Then we'll follow you."

The children sat still while Diego inched his way toward the rear of the plane. In a few moments he had unlocked the small door. He squeezed through. Then, grasping the tail with both hands, he hung from it.

"Okay!" he yelled.

One by one, Mr. Vega had the children crawl out slowly, then followed himself.

"I'm very sorry to have given you all such a fright," he said.

"It wasn't your fault," Holly spoke up. "It was the dogie's."

"What's a dogie?" Sue asked, perplexed.

Dolores explained that it is a little orphan calf. "Sometimes they wander away from their mothers and get lost on the range."

"Then what happens?" Holly queried, worried about the one they had nearly run down.

"Sometimes they die from thirst or are attacked by mountain lions," Dolores replied.

"Oh, I hope we can find that dogie again and take it to its mother," Sue spoke up.

Meanwhile, Mr. Vega and the boys had started to examine the plane. The right front wheel was out of alignment and the propeller was broken.

"The plane can't fly with a broken propeller, can it?" Ricky asked.

"That's right," Mr. Vega answered.

"Then how are we going to get home?" the boy asked.

"If we can fix the wheel, Dad," Diego spoke up, "couldn't we taxi back to the ranch house?"

"It's possible, son. But we might have to cut a path in places."

"We might try it, though."

Mr. Vega went to the edge of the *arroyo* and looked at the wheel.

"First of all," he said, "we'll have to get that wheel back on level ground. Suppose all of you but Sue and Holly come and help me."

As the children pulled and tugged at the plane, the two little girls walked away. Sue kept glancing around anxiously, and to her sister's surprise, tears began to roll down her face.

"What's the matter?" Holly asked her.

"That poor lost dogie," Sue said. "We must find it before a lion or something gets it. Come on, let's hunt for it. Will you help me, Holly?"

"Of course," Holly said, giving the smaller girl a hug. "Did you see which way it went?"

Sue pointed to where she had seen the animal disappear over a knoll of high piñon bushes and rabbit brush. Holly took her sister by the hand and they walked off in search of the lost dogie.

Back at the edge of the *arroyo*, Mr. Vega and his helpers were having difficulty dragging the plane out of the gully.

"Will you help me hunt for the lost dogie?"

At the man's request, Ricky had climbed inside the ship to get two strong lassos. Diego took them. Lying down flat on the ground near the rim of the *arroyo*, he tied the ropes to the right front wheel.

"Fine," Mr. Vega said. "Now let's all take hold of these ropes. Then when I count to three, pull. Ready?" he asked a moment later.

"Ready."

"One, two, *three!*"

Tugging with all their might, the children managed to move the plane an inch.

"It's coming!" Pete cried.

"All right. Let's try again," Mr. Vega urged.

Again the six of them pulled together. Inch by inch the wheel came up over the edge of the *arroyo*, until the plane finally rested level.

"We made it!" Diego shouted joyously.

"Well done, crew," Mr. Vega praised the children, as everyone pushed the plane farther back from the dangerous spot.

When it had been wheeled to a good location for taxiing it home, Mr. Vega examined the twisted wheel. He declared this could be remedied in a jiffy and asked Pete to bring him some tools.

"You girls may as well get inside," he said.

Pam and Dolores suddenly realized that they were the only girls there. Sue and Holly were not in sight.

"Holly! Sue! Come back! We're going home now!" Pam called at the top of her lungs. There was no reply.

"I see Sue's and Holly's footprints. Come on!"

"Where could they have gone?" the girl murmured, worried.

"Maybe they're looking for the dogie," Dolores suggested.

She took up the cry. When the boys realized the little girls were not answering, they shouted lustily. Still there was no sound from the missing children.

"This is a bad place to get lost in," Diego said. "All these *arroyos* and bushes will make it hard to find them out there."

Ricky had wandered off a little way and suddenly yelled, "I see Sue's and Holly's footprints. Come on, let's follow them!"

Everybody hurried after the boy. The marks the little girls had left were quite clear until they reached a stony *arroyo* on the other side of the knoll. There the tracks suddenly disappeared. The search continued, however, for two hours. By this time shadows had begun to lengthen.

"It'll be dark before long," Pam groaned, frantic with worry.

"It gets cold out here on the prairie at night, too!" Diego whispered to his sister.

Mr. Vega was grim. How could he ever face Mr. and Mrs. Hollister if anything had happened to their little girls?

"But I mustn't give up hope," he determined as dusk settled over the valley.

As he stood lost in thought, wondering what to do next—perhaps notify the police on the plane's radio— Pete came up to him.

"Mr. Vega," he said, "have you a flashlight in the plane?"

"Yes," he replied.

"That might help us find the girls," Pete told him. "A light carries farther than our voices. If we keep flashing it off and on, Holly and Sue will see the beam and come toward it."

"A very good idea," Mr. Vega said.

The sun had already settled behind the rim of the peak Pete thought was Mystery Mountain and it grew dark quickly. The searchers hurried back to the plane, where Diego got a large flashlight from the tool compartment.

"It's dark enough to start flashing this right now," he said.

He flicked it on and off for half an hour. Every once in a while the group would shout. But nothing happened.

"May I have the light?" Pete asked. "I have another idea. Maybe the girls ran along the bottom of the *arroyo* where we lost the footprints."

"And we haven't searched there!" Diego exclaimed. "Our voices might have carried right over the top!"

Mr. Vega thought it best if they divided forces. There was a smaller flashlight in the plane, which he said he would keep waving where they were. Ricky, Dolores, and Pam had better stay with him.

They were sleeping with a baby lamb.

"And you boys be mighty careful in your search," he insisted. "Keep your eyes and ears open to every sound. There are plenty of animals roaming around at night."

Pete and Diego set off and hurried along the floor of the deep *arroyo* in a northerly direction. They had gone about a mile when Pete, in the lead and flashing the big light, said excitedly:

"Look! Ahead there! It might be—"

Without finishing the sentence, Pete dashed forward, running pell-mell across the boulders and tough clumps of grass. Suddenly he stopped short and broke into a hearty laugh. Diego too chuckled in relief.

Before them, nestled on the ground, their heads close together, were Holly and Sue, sound asleep. And between them lay a woolly baby lamb!

The laughter awakened the little girls. Looking up into the beam of the flashlight, they rubbed their eyes.

"Hi, Pete!" Holly said cheerfully, not a bit disturbed at having been lost.

"Isn't our lamb 'dorable?" Sue asked, hugging it.

The girls arose. The lamb got up too, and bleated a couple of times.

"I'll see if it's one of ours," Diego said. He bent over the animal and looked at her ears. On the left one was a daub of red paint.

"This lamb is ours, all right!" the boy said excitedly. "Where did you find it?"

Holly explained that while she and Sue were looking for the dogie, they had heard the pitiful bleating of the lost lamb in the *arroyo*.

"We called to it," said Sue, "and it came right up to us."

"We'd better hurry back to the plane," Pete said. "Can you girls walk or are you too tired?"

"We're all right."

Diego suggested that walking would be easier on the ground above the *arroyo* and he knew a short cut that might save a quarter of a mile.

Some distance from the plane, Pete began to shout, "We found them! They're all right!"

"Oh, that's wonderful!" Pam called back, and ran to meet them.

There were hugs and kisses. Finally, Mr. Vega's voice could be heard saying:

"We must let our families know where we are."

"How will we do that?" Ricky asked.

"There's a two-way radio in the plane. I can tune it to the police station at Sunrise. I hope the set wasn't damaged by our accident."

As he walked toward the ship, Pete found a piece of wood and drove it into the ground. Then he tied one of the lassos around the lamb's neck and hitched her to the stake.

The other children had followed Mr. Vega into the plane to watch him send the message. He switched on the button and spoke into the microphone.

"Calling Sunrise police. Calling Sunrise police. This is Frank Vega calling Sunrise police."

The children waited silently. Would the message get through?

CHAPTER 10

Animal Orphans

"THIS is the Sunrise police," a voice crackled over the loud-speaker.

"Frank Vega speaking."

The rancher told of their predicament and their location. "We'll be all right here for the night," he said. "Please tell my wife and the Hollisters where we are. And ask Truchas to come for us tomorrow morning with horses in case we can't taxi the plane out."

"Tell Daddy to come, too," Sue called. Mr. Vega smiled and delivered this message.

The police promised to get in touch with the ranch house, then Mr. Vega switched off the radio and turned to the children.

"How about some chow?" he asked. "If you're as hungry as I am, you could eat a Texas steer."

As the others giggled, he said, "Dolores, suppose you play mother tonight. You know where the emergency rations are, don't you?"

"Sure, Daddy, I'll fix something right away."

As the Hollister children watched, she went to the back of the plane and opened a small compartment. Inside it were many cans of food.

"What would you like to have?" Dolores said as she pulled them out. "Chili con carne or baked beans?"

Pam said they had tried chili con carne on their way to New Mexico and thought it a bit peppery.

"I'll take beans," she said, and the other Hollisters decided on this too.

"And canned peaches for dessert?" Dolores asked.

"Yummy!" exclaimed Sue.

"Let's make a fire to heat the beans, instead of using the canned heat," Diego suggested.

"Yes, that'll be more fun," his sister agreed.

Diego climbed out of the plane. Ricky followed him and together the boys gathered enough brushwood to start a cheery blaze. Holly found a pan in the compartment and also a can opener. She went outside with Pam, who carried a box of crackers and some tin plates to the place where the fire was already crackling.

Pete had stayed in the plane to speak to Mr. Vega, who was examining the instrument panel.

"Is there a railroad near by?" he asked the rancher.

"Yes, there is, not many miles away."

"Is there a loading platform on the railroad?" the boy asked.

"Yes. Why do you ask?"

"I have an idea," Pete said. "Maybe the sheep rustler took the animals to the railroad and shipped them off. The lamb Holly and Sue found might have escaped while he was doing this."

"M-m, that smells good!"

"That's possible," Mr. Vega said. "A very plausible idea. The loading platform is old and not used much. A rustler might easily arrange to have a cattle train stop there without the railroad becoming suspicious."

"What place do sheep from here go?" asked Pete.

"Kansas City."

Before Pete and Mr. Vega could discuss the subject further, Dolores poked her head into the plane.

"Supper's ready!" she called.

"That's good," said Pete. "I'm hungry."

At the blazing campfire, beans and chili con carne were steaming in the cans. Diego scooped them onto the plates and Dolores handed them around.

"M-m, that smells good!" Pam said, as she passed crackers.

As they all started to eat, Sue wanted to know if there was any milk.

"Why yes," Dolores replied. "I forgot all about it."

She opened several cans and mixed the contents with water.

"This is just like cow's milk," Sue stated, and the others laughed, because it *was* cow's milk.

Suddenly Pam exclaimed, "Ooo-oh!"

Pete jumped involuntarily. "What's the matter?" he asked.

"I just saw the most beautiful meteor flash across the sky," his sister replied.

The children looked up into the starlit sky, but the meteor had passed. The heavens, however, were like a sparkling dome, extending from one horizon to the other.

"Wow! Don't frighten us like that again," Diego chuckled.

When the meal was over, the campers continued to sit around the fire and started to sing songs. When they came to "Home on the Range," with the words *Where the deer and the antelope play*, Sue began to look around into the darkness. Her head turned this way and that.

"What are you looking for?" Dolores asked her.

"I want to see the deer and the antelope playing," the little girl explained.

The others laughed and the ranch girl said that the animals were asleep.

"And you should be too," Pam told her small sister, as Sue yawned.

Pam had heard a faint cry!

"Are we going to sleep inside the plane?" Holly asked.

"I guess some of us will have to," Mr. Vega replied. "There aren't enough blankets for all of us. Diego and I will stay out here and keep watch. The rest of you go inside."

Before long the younger children were fast asleep, curled up on the chairs. Pete, Pam, and Dolores stretched out on the carpeted floor.

In the middle of the night Pam awakened and sat bolt upright, her eyes wide. Had she heard a noise like a faint cry? She listened, as her heart pounded. The sound came again. It was outside the plane.

Had something happened to Diego or Mr. Vega?

Pam touched her brother's arm. "Pete, wake up!"

As her brother roused sleepily, she told him her fears.

"I think we'd better go outside and investigate," the boy said.

Pete still had one of the flashlights with him. He snapped it on and led the way. Diego and his father were sound asleep.

"They weren't bothered by the noise," Pam remarked softly.

"It must be something that's natural to the range," Pete whispered. "Otherwise it would have disturbed them."

"Just the same I'd like to find out what it was," Pam said. "Listen! There's the cry again!"

It seemed to come from a distance on the other side of the plane. As Pam moved toward it, Pete held her back.

"Be careful!" he warned. "It might be Mesquite Mike prowling around and trying to fool us by making a sound like an animal."

"You're not going alone," his sister told him as he pushed ahead of her.

Together the children tiptoed to the far side of the plane, Pete flashing the light.

In its beam the piñon bushes and scrubby cedars cast long, spooky shadows. But nobody was in sight.

"Maybe someone's hiding behind the bushes," Pete suggested. "Let's find out."

Walking softly, he focused the light among the piñons and also behind several large boulders which lay near by. All at once the children heard the whimpering cry again.

"Now I know where it's coming from!" Pete exclaimed.

"I do too," said Pam. "The place where the lamb is tied."

"That's why the Vegas didn't bother about it," Pete whispered.

"But maybe somebody's trying to steal the lamb again!" Pam worried.

Cautiously she approached the spot where the lamb was tied to the stake, while Pete flashed his light around. The beam found the white lamb, who lay huddled on the ground. But it also picked up another animal.

Pam uttered a cry before she realized what it was. Then the girl and her brother burst out laughing.

"It's the lost dogie!" Pam exclaimed. "Licking the lamb's face and trying to cuddle down with it!"

"It's the lost dogie!"

The laughter and loud talking awakened Mr. Vega and Diego, who came running to the spot. When they were sure the children were all right, the father and son gazed at the little scene and chuckled.

"Just a couple of orphans," Diego said.

The children walked forward and this time the dogie did not run away. Nevertheless they all thought it best to tie the calf.

There were no more disturbances the rest of the night. It was not until Sue shouted "Get up, you sleepy-heads!" that they realized it was morning.

"Oh, look, it's Monday!" cried the little girl, who was looking out a window of the plane.

Pam turned drowsily. Sue, she thought, was always getting her days mixed up. This was not Monday. It was— But suddenly Pam heard the other children exclaiming. She got up and looked out.

There was Monday, the burro. On his back was Truchas. Following Monday came Tuesday, Wednesday, Thursday, Friday, Saturday, and Sunday, plodding along in single file.

"Hurray, we're rescued!" Ricky shouted, as he scampered out of the plane and ran to meet Truchas.

CHAPTER 11

The Herder's Secret

TRUCHAS grinned as Ricky hurried toward him and the burros.

"So the plane cracked up, eh?" he teased. "Burros never break a propeller. And they don't run out o' gasoline. I'll stick to burros."

"I guess I will too," said Ricky. "May I ride one home all alone?"

"Well, son, we'll see how Mr. Vega's goin' to arrange things," the sheepherder answered. "Maybe we'll have to double up."

By this time everybody was talking excitedly.

"You made good time, Truchas," Mr. Vega praised him.

"Guess I did," the old man answered. "My burros can make better time than a jeep too. I beat Mr. Hollister gettin' here."

Mr. Vega laughed. "By knowing all the short cuts and going in and out of the *arroyos*," he said.

He had hardly finished speaking when they heard the distant hum of a motor and presently Mr. Hollister drew up and stopped. He looked unbelievingly at Truchas and the burros.

"My burros go faster than jeeps!"

"You must have a magic carpet," he chuckled.

"I've got magic mules," the old man answered proudly.

Mr. Vega suggested that as soon as they had all had breakfast from supplies Truchas had brought, the herder take the children home. He and Mr. Hollister would see what they could do with the plane. While eating, Pete said to the ranch owner:

"May I report to the police that maybe your stolen sheep were shipped on the railroad to Kansas City?"

"I'd rather you wire the stockyard in Kansas City direct," Mr. Vega said. "I'll leave it to you and Diego to take care of the matter."

"All aboard the burros!" Truchas' voice rang out, and Mr. Vega helped the children onto the backs of the friendly little animals.

Sue was to ride in front of Truchas. Each of the others would have a burro to himself.

"Aren't we going to take the lamb and the dogie?" Pam spoke up.

"Oh yes, I nearly forgot them," said Dolores.

"I want to have the dogie walk behind me," Ricky announced, and ran to get the little animal, who was grazing.

Truchas went to look at the young calf. "There's no brand mark on him, Mr. Vega," he said, "so I suppose we can take him along."

The sheepherder explained to the Hollisters that unbranded cattle sometimes roamed the range and belonged to whoever found them.

Holly lifted up the lamb and laid the animal across the burro in front of her. The little band started off, with Truchas in the lead and Pete bringing up the rear on Domingo.

Up and down the hills they went, when suddenly Holly asked in surprise, "Dolores, who gave this lamb chewing gum?"

"Chewing gum!" Dolores exclaimed with a giggle. "Nobody."

"Well, the lamb is chewing something," Holly insisted.

"She's chewing her cud," Diego explained, smiling.

"I thought only cows did that," Holly said, a little embarrassed.

"Sheep do too," Dolores added, as the little group stopped to let the Hollister children observe the woolly animal.

Diego grinned. "Sheep have four stomachs, you know. When they graze, the food goes into one of their stomachs. Then it comes back into their mouths and they chew it some more before swallowing it again."

"That's keen!" Ricky piped up. "Then they can eat all day long."

"You'd make a good lamb!" said Pam, joking with her brother. "Dad says you have two hollow legs and that's why Mother can't fill you up."

After they had watched the lamb chew the cud for a while and were about to set off again, Sue pursed her lips and said sadly, "I really feel sorry for lambies."

"Why?" Dolores asked.

"Who gave this lamb chewing gum?"

" 'Cause they can get four tummy aches. I only get one, and that's bad enough."

Everybody laughed as they went along, which made the time pass quickly. After they had ridden for another hour, the riders came to the top of a small hill.

"I see the buildings of Cottonwood Ranch!" Ricky shouted, pointing.

As the burro train wound up to the ranch house, Mrs. Hollister and Mrs. Vega rushed out to meet them.

"Thank goodness all of you are safe!" Mrs. Hollister exclaimed, as she lifted Sue from the burro and hugged her. "And where did you get these babies?" she asked, seeing the lamb and the dogie.

"Oh, they're orphans," said Holly, "and they're going to live with us."

She went off with Pam and Dolores to put the lamb in a pen until the little orphan could be taken to a herd. Ricky led the dogie to another one. While this was going on, Pete and Diego helped Truchas wipe off and stable the burros.

Finally the old man called Ricky, Holly, and Sue into a little private conference. After he had talked a few minutes, Sue began to bob her head vigorously.

" 'Course I can keep a secret," she maintained. Giggling, she added, "This is an orphan secret!"

"What's going on?" Pam called.

"Can't tell you—yet," Holly answered.

The others did not tease to know what the secret was and the two older boys ran into the house. They went at once to the telephone with the intention of sending a telegram through the Sunrise office. But Diego was unable to get the operator.

"It's out of order I guess," he said. "We'll have to give it up and drive to town," he told Pete. "We'll take the truck and ask Truchas to go along."

He spoke to his mother, who gave her consent, and the boys hurried off to find the herder. At first the old man did not seem interested and said he preferred waiting until the plane came back. But when he heard about the telegram, Truchas said he would accompany the boys.

Diego ran into the garage and backed the truck into the yard. When Pete saw him do this, his eyes grew wide.

"Can kids drive cars out here?" he asked.

"Can kids drive cars out here?"

Diego explained that the Western boys learned to drive cars at an early age because they helped on the ranches.

Diego kept the wheel until they reached the public highway, then Truchas slid into the driver's seat. When they arrived at Sunrise, the herder pulled up to the curb and parked. He said he would meet the boys in half an hour. As they started off, Diego said, "The telegraph office is down the street. We'll send the message right away."

Before they reached it, the boys passed a shop that sold men's clothing. Suddenly Pete grabbed Diego's arm.

"Look in there!" he said excitedly.

Diego gave a low whistle. "What do you know about that?" he said.

Near the front of the store stood Mesquite Mike trying on a new ten-gallon hat!

"That proves to me it was his old one we found in the *arroyo*," Pete declared. Then he whispered, "Diego, you send the telegram and I'll trail Mesquite Mike. Maybe I can learn something."

"Okay. If I don't see you, I'll meet you at the car."

Pete slipped into an alleyway and watched for the cowboy to come out. In a few minutes he came from the shop, wearing the new hat, and swaggered down the street in the opposite direction.

Like a detective, Pete was right after him. Mesquite Mike walked the full length of the main street without looking back. Then he turned a corner and set off toward a group of rather shabby one-story dwellings with boxes and cans scattered about untidily. Reaching the last house, he knocked on the door. It was opened and he went in.

"Maybe I'd better tell the police," Pete thought, as he hid himself behind a large carton so that the man would not see him if he should look out a window.

Before he had a chance, the door opened and the man came out. But he was no longer wearing the new hat. Mesquite Mike had changed to an older one.

"I wonder if that's his?" Pete said to himself. "Or did he borrow it?"

The cowboy walked toward the open country to where a saddled pony was grazing. Mesquite swung into the saddle and rode off.

Pete was curious to learn who lived in the house where the man had stopped. Seeing a little boy come out of another, he asked him.

"Willie Boot and his mother live there," the boy answered. "But Willie's not home much."

"He's with Mesquite Mike a lot, isn't he?" Pete prodded the child, who said his name was Stan.

"Yes. But I'm kind of scared of Mike."

"Why?"

"He tells us awful stories about stampedes and things," Stan replied. "He knows how to cut out cattle and rope 'em and—"

"Willie's not home."

As the lad paused, Pete asked him if Mesquite ever talked about sheep and whether he knew a lot about them, too.

"Sure he does," the boy answered.

Though Pete asked Stan several other questions he could not find out anything damaging to the cowboy. If he were a rustler, he had kept his secret well.

"I don't like Willie either," Stan said. "He takes our toys."

At this moment Stan's mother called him and he ran off. Pete walked back toward the car, thinking hard about what he had just heard. Neither Truchas nor Diego was there so Pete went to the telegraph office. Inside, Diego was seated at a little desk that had a pencil chained on top of it. His telegram read:

MANAGER
KANSAS CITY STOCKYARD
ABOUT TWENTY-FIVE SHEEP WITH VEGA MARK MAY HAVE BEEN SHIPPED TO MARKET WITHIN PAST WEEK BY RUSTLER. PLEASE REPLY.

D. VEGA
SUNRISE

After giving the message to the man at the counter, Diego paid for it, then the boys walked out. At once Pete explained that he had learned where Willie Boot lived and what Stan had told him about Mesquite.

"I'm convinced he has been taking the sheep," Pete concluded.

"And maybe Willie helped him!" Diego suggested. Then suddenly he exclaimed, "Jumping bullfrogs! Look at that!" He pointed across the street.

Walking along were Jack and Helen Moore and with them, chatting in a very friendly fashion, was Willie Boot!

"Well, I'll be a gopher!" Diego said. "I thought you told me the Moores didn't have any use for Willie Boot!"

CHAPTER 12

A Watery Spill

PETE was dumbfounded to find Jack and Helen Moore with Willie Boot. "It doesn't make sense," he said to Diego. "I'm going to find out what it's all about."

Running across the street with Diego after him, he called out, "Hi, Jack! Hi, Helen! How's everything at the dude ranch?"

The Moore children were surprised to see Pete and asked how Pam and the others were. Then Pete introduced the Moores to Diego.

"And this is Willie Boot," Helen said to him.

"I know Willie," Diego said without enthusiasm.

Pete asked if anything had been learned at the Bishops' Ranch about their stolen sheep but Jack shook his head. Pete kept watching Willie out of the corner of his eye but that boy kept a stony look and did not act as if he knew anything about it.

"I suppose you're wondering why we're with Willie," Helen said. "We met him in town this morning and asked him if he took our old book on Mexico," she said.

"I didn't steal it, honest," Willie spoke up.

"I guess we'll have to take his word for it," Jack said.

With this, Willie started to move off. But Pete took hold of his shoulder. "Just a minute, Willie. If you expect us to believe that, you'll have to tell us one thing."

"What's that?"

"Where Mesquite Mike lives."

Willie looked at the ground and kicked some of the sandy soil with his foot. He asked why they wanted to know, and Pete countered with:

"If you have nothing to hide, why won't you tell us?"

"Okay," the boy said. "Mike told me he just moved into a place out of town along the river. It's hidden by the trees." Willie began to walk off, then stopped a moment. "Say, don't you tell Mike I told you. He—he might whip me!"

Pete promised. Then, after Willie was gone, he urged the Moores to go with him and have a talk with Mesquite Mike.

"Maybe we ought to get a policeman," Helen said a little fearfully.

"All right," the boys agreed.

While Jack and Helen went into the local head-quarters, Pete and Diego hurried to the truck and told Truchas where they were going.

"I'm all for it," the old man said. "Jump in."

He drove to the police station and picked up the Moores and a friendly young officer to whom they had told their whole story. Grinning, he said:

"You children surely are great detectives! We've been suspicious of Mesquite for more than a year and have been trying to investigate his hide-out. If we could only find things we think he stole we could arrest him. But he keeps changing his hide-out all the time."

"Didn't you question him?" Helen asked.

"Oh yes, we did," the policeman replied. "Mike insisted he was honest and said he camped under the stars. But we figured he had a hut somewhere."

"Well, now you know," Pete said proudly. "Are you going to search it?"

The officer grinned. "Sure enough. I'll get a warrant. Wait for me outside."

A few minutes later they were on their way to look for Mesquite's place. Since there were only two small wooded sections along the river on the outskirts of Sunrise, they could narrow their search immediately.

The first of the woods they inspected was used mainly for a picnic ground. It had rusted tables and

They started their search for Mesquite.

benches and several small fireplaces. The only spot where anybody could possibly live was a small tree house which Diego spied.

"Suppose he could live up there?" the ranch boy asked.

"I'll take a look," Pete replied. As the officer smiled at the nimble boy, Pete shinned up to the lowest limb and soon was peering into the tree house.

"Nobody lives here but a noisy magpie," Pete called out as an excited bird settled on a limb above him.

But as Pete started to climb down, his eyes settled on some strange marks pressed into the floor of the hut. He looked harder and found more.

"Hey, did you find anything?" the officer called up.

"Yes. Somebody wearing spurs has been up here!" Pete exclaimed.

In a few seconds the officer was beside the boy. "You're right," he said excitedly.

"I'll bet Mesquite used this as a lookout!" Pete reasoned. "His place must be near by. Let's go!"

After they scrambled down the tree, Pete and the officer led the group to the second woods. It was full of gnarled old trees and was crisscrossed with heavy vines.

"No shacks here," Jack groaned. "Willie told us a fib."

"Nobody's home!"

"Wait," Diego said, his sharp eyes glancing at the base of an ancient cottonwood tree. "That's an awful big hole for an animal to make."

"More like a human coyote," Pete observed.

The officer agreed. "I'm going to take a look into this. If it's Mesquite's hide-out, we won't need the search warrant because this is not a home!"

The policeman lighted a match and peered into the hole. "Right you are!" he exclaimed. "This is an underground hut. Nobody's home."

As he crawled inside and lighted a candle stuck into the earthen wall, the others followed. The place was full of boxes and newspapers. On a cot in one corner of the room lay a stack of magazines and a few old books. Helen went over and picked up the top book.

"My stolen book!" she cried out. "Willie didn't take it. Mesquite Mike was the one!"

Helen asked the officer if she might keep the book.

"Of course you may," he replied. "And when Mike gets back, I'll take him in on a charge of petty larceny."

Helen had started to thumb through the old book. She wanted to see the sketch of Mystery Mountain. But when she came to the chapter on the dollmakers, the girl exclaimed:

"The sketch has been torn out!"

"Mesquite Mike has gone off to find Mystery Mountain!" Jack groaned.

"Then we ought to go after him!" Pete declared.

"But how?" Helen asked.

"Maybe Mike didn't take the page with him," the officer suggested. "Let's look around."

A hunt began. The page did not show up but Pete did find a crumpled sheet on which was drawn a crude map.

"Maybe this tells how to get to Mystery Mountain!" the boy said excitedly.

The officer looked at it, saying he doubted that the drawing was any good. Nevertheless Pete put the paper into his pocket.

After they got back to town and the officer had left them, Jack and Helen said that they were going to start off the next morning to hunt for Mystery Mountain. They proposed making a party of it. How about Pete, Pam, and Diego joining them?

"I'd sure like to," Pete answered, "and I know Pam would. How about you, Diego?"

"Sorry," the ranch boy replied. "Tomorrow's my day to ride fence."

Pete promised to let the Moores know if his parents would consent. Should the Vegas' telephone not be working, he would ride over and tell them.

"What time will you start?" he asked.

"Nine o'clock."

"Okay, Pam and I'll be there by then."

"Will you bring lunch, Pete?" Helen asked. "We'll pack one."

Pete said he would, then the Moores waved good-by.

"I wish you were going tomorrow, Diego," Pete said as Truchas drove off.

"I'm afraid I can't get out of my job," the boy answered.

As the three drove up to the ranch buildings some time later, they noticed Ricky ambling toward the dogie, who was now staked to a rope in the field.

"Directions to Mystery Mountain!"

"What's he up to?" Pete wondered.

His brother went up to the animal and gently patted his head. Then quickly he untied the dogie and sprang onto the animal's back. The calf was so surprised that at first he did not move.

"Giddap!" Ricky commanded.

Suddenly the calf leaped forward. The boy clung to his neck so he would stay on. Away the calf went around the barnyard, running and bucking and trying to throw his rider to the ground. But Ricky dug his knees in and hung on.

Suddenly the dogie stopped short, as if he had been struck by a bright idea. Then he set off again at a furious gait and headed directly toward a trough filled with water for the farm animals.

All at once the calf stiffened his four legs and skidded to a sudden halt. Ricky went flying over his head into the water!

Pete sprang forward to help his brother but this was not necessary. Ricky rose, dripping wet and spluttering water from his mouth and nose.

"I know a good name for the dogie," Pete chuckled.

"What? Bronco?" Diego asked, grinning.

"No. Let's call him Dunker. Ricky sure was dunked into the water."

As the dripping boy walked toward the ranch house to change his clothes, Diego went off to capture the calf.

Meanwhile Truchas had put the truck away and now came over to where the children were standing. Holly and Sue had joined them.

"Don't you think we ought to do the secret now?" Sue asked the old herder.

The man took off his sombrero and scratched his head, as if this would help him to decide what to answer. Finally he said:

"You got a point there, señorita. I was going to wait till the jeep came back, but I guess we can use the truck."

Sue jumped up and down, clapping her hands excitedly. Holly pulled Truchas' head down near her mouth and whispered something to him. He grinned and said aloud:

"I guess we can't keep this a secret any longer. Well, who wants to tell it?"

Each of the little girls wanted to but felt that it would not be fair until Ricky got back. They did not have long to wait because their brother had changed his clothes in a very few minutes. As he ran up to the group, Sue said:

"We're allowed to tell the secret now. I want to be the one."

"All right, go ahead," Ricky agreed, and Holly nodded.

CHAPTER 13

Home on the Range

"WHAT'S the big secret?" Pam asked her younger brother and sisters.

Sue stood up very straight and announced, "Truchas is going to let Holly and Ricky and me go with him and give the babies back to their mothers."

Pam laughed and asked what she meant by this. Holly explained that the three children were going to deliver the dogie and the baby lamb to the herds from which they had been lost.

"But I thought we decided," Pete spoke up, "that the sheep were stolen and probably are on their way to Kansas City."

Truchas said that it would not matter which herd the baby lamb was given to. She could take care of herself as long as she had some protection from the older animals.

"How soon can we go?" Ricky wanted to know.

"As soon as we get the truck gassed up and your mother says you can go."

As Pam listened a wistful look came into her face. This sounded like an exciting adventure and she wished she might go along. Truchas must have read

The calf bawled loudly.

her thoughts because he suddenly smiled at the girl and invited her to accompany them.

"Oh, thank you!" she cried. "I'll ask Mother."

When Mrs. Hollister heard the plan, she consulted Mrs. Vega about it.

"Oh, it's perfectly safe," the ranch woman replied. "Truchas will take good care of them."

Since there was only one seat in the truck, Diego fitted a plank into the vehicle just behind the cab and spread an old carpet over it as a second seat. The baby animals were hobbled, then hoisted into the back and tied to the sides of the truck so they could not move.

"All aboard!" Truchas called out.

The four Hollister children climbed aboard. Sue sat next to Truchas, with Ricky on the end. Pam and Holly took the rear seat.

What a din there was as the truck started off! The dog Beans barked joyfully. But the lamb and the dogie made it known that they did not like the treatment they were getting. The calf bawled loudly and the lamb gave a series of pitiful *baas!*

Everybody laughed except Sue. She was very serious. Kneeling on the seat and looking back, she said, "Don't cry! We're not going to hurt you."

After a long ride they saw cattle grazing on a slope. Truchas drove directly to them and stopped. As the old man stepped out of the truck, he said:

"Well, here's where we leave the dogie. Come on, you young cowboys, help me get 'im out of here."

The children climbed to the rear of the truck and helped the herder untie the knots of the ropes which bound the calf. Then they lifted him to the ground. Like a shot he loped toward the older animals, going from one to another and rubbing noses with them.

"He's kissing them!" Sue called out gleefully.

"The dogie is certainly glad to be back," Holly remarked. "Truchas, are you sure they'll be nice to him?"

The herder nodded, and with this assurance the children got back into the truck and rode away.

"Do we have far to go now?" Pam asked.

"It's quite a way," Truchas answered. "Sometimes we keep cattle and sheep close together because sheep aren't fighters and the calves will drive off enemies. But at this time of year the sheep like high ground."

"Why?" Holly asked.

Truchas tilted his sombrero, and his leathery face wrinkled as he grinned at the girl. "You'd do well in a 4-H Club!" he said, and before Holly could ask a question about that, the old herder went on:

"Sheep like higher ground because there's better pasture for them. More nice weeds to eat. Besides, sheep originally came from high countries, so they're right at home near the clouds!"

Sue giggled. "How much longer do we have to ride to get near the clouds, Truchas?"

They wished the board seat had cushions on it.

" 'Bout an hour," the herder replied. Then he chuckled. "Do you think you can stand it?"

The children said stoutly that they could. But secretly each one was thinking that he had never been so uncomfortable on a ride before. Pam and Holly particularly wished there were a back to their board seat and that it had some cushions on it!

"It won't be long now," Truchas announced finally. "If you children will keep your eyes open, you'll see the sheep over to the left on that hill."

Presently white dots became visible and soon they were driving up to one of the herds which the children had seen from the air. Truchas stopped at the foot of the hill and they all climbed out.

"What fine-looking lambs!" Pam said as her gaze drifted over the flock.

"Glad you like 'em," Truchas said, his eyes squinting. "Best two-year-olds on the range."

"Are they only two?" Sue asked, wide-eyed. "How can you tell?"

"By their size—and their teeth!" came the reply.

At this all the Hollisters turned to the old herder with questioning looks.

"All right, all right!" Truchas chuckled, holding up his hands as if to ward off an outburst of queries. "I'll tell you about their teeth."

"Are you a lambie dentist?" Sue piped up.

"Shush!" Pam said. "No, he's not. Let Truchas tell his story."

Sue held her hands behind her back and swayed from one foot to the other. The kind old man went on:

"A sheep has eight front teeth, all in the lower jaw. These come up against a rubber-like pad in the upper jaw."

"Tsk-tsk!" Holly burst out. "Don't they ever get teeth upstairs?"

"Not in front!" the herder replied, rubbing his hand over his chin. "Now, about their age. A lamb gets its eight front teeth by the time it's three weeks old. It may have two or four at birth."

Sue put her fingers in her mouth. "Pam," she said thickly, "did I have any teeth when I was born?"

Pam laughed. "No, honey."

Truchas grinned too. "And sheep get all their second teeth before you start losing your first ones," he said. "They're all set when they're only four years old to eat the toughest kind of grass."

At this moment the lamb in the truck bleated. Sue looked at it tenderly and asked:

"She's crying. When are we going to make our lambie not an orphan?"

Everybody grinned and turned toward the tied-up baby sheep. "Right now," Truchas promised. "Actually she's smiling. The lamb knows she's near a herd," the man added, as Ricky untied the little animal and set her on the ground.

"Now you won't be an orphan any more," Sue told her, giving the animal a good-by hug. "You'll have lots of mothers and fathers."

The lamb bounded toward her family.

Holly looked very sad as she too hugged the lamb. "I'll probably never see you again," she said. "But I'll always remember you. Take good care of yourself."

The little animal paused a couple of seconds and suddenly rubbed her nose against those of Holly and Sue. The little girls giggled, then released the animal, who bounded forward to her sheep family.

"Good-by! Good-by!" all the children called, as they watched her gambol up the hillside and disappear among the larger animals.

"Oh, this was such fun!" Pam said, as they stepped into the truck and started for home.

"It sure was," said Ricky. Looking directly at Truchas, he added, "I don't want to be a dude. I want to be a real cowboy or a sheepherder."

Truchas smiled. "Tell you what, son," he said. "You try it for a while in Shoreham and if you don't like it there, get your daddy to send you out here and I'll take you under my wing."

At this moment Ricky was quite sure he would return to the Vegas' ranch before very long. He became so lost in thought that the next thing he knew, the truck was within sight of the ranch buildings.

"Oh, look!" Pam called out. "There's Daddy driving the jeep and towing the airplane with Mr. Vega inside."

As soon as Truchas parked the truck, the children got out and ran over to the men. After telling about their adventure, Ricky said:

"Mr. Vega, how are you going to get your plane fixed?"

"Oh, we can make the repairs right here," Mr. Vega answered. "On a ranch one has to learn to be a good mechanic. We have a well-equipped tool shop here in one end of the barn. Come, I'll show it to you."

The two went off, while the others walked to the house, but in a few moments Mr. Vega and Ricky joined them. The little boy's eyes were glowing and he declared that the workshop had even more tools than the Trading Post.

"Then it has an awful lot," said Pete.

At this moment the telephone rang. Diego answered it.

"Your line has been repaired," a voice said, "and there's a telegram for you from Kansas City."

"Will you please read it to me?" Diego asked.

The boy listened intently for a few moments, a perplexed look coming over his face. Then he said, "Thank you," and hung up.

"Dad!" he called to his father, who was just entering the room. "Kansas City hasn't received any of our sheep lately."

"Then your animals may still be somewhere on the range!" Pete reasoned. "If the lost sheep are on Cottonwood Ranch," he added to Diego after Mr. Vega had gone out, "we certainly ought to find them!"

"Right," Diego agreed. "I'll keep my eyes open while I'm riding fence tomorrow."

Ricky, who had been listening intently, sidled up to him. "Will you take me along?" he requested.

"Why sure, if you can stand it."

"Just what do you do?" the smaller boy asked.

"Well, sometimes the fences that separate our property from neighbors, break, and we have to mend them so that our cattle can't wander off."

"Don't the steers ever jump over?" Ricky asked.

Diego said this was rare. "Cattle are pretty slow-thinking and content. As long as they have enough to eat and drink, they stay inside the fence.

"But sheep are different," he added. "We can't fence them in and they wander all around. We use dogs to help the herdsmen keep them together."

At dusk that evening Mrs. Hollister called the roll for her children to prepare for bed. When she did this at home in Shoreham the children giggled and gave

funny answers, like *Ricky is sticky and can't go to bed.*
This evening Holly chirped, "Pam is a woolly lamb
and will be a dolly for Holly's bed."

Suddenly Pete said, "Say, where's Sue? I haven't
heard a peep out of that little cricket."

"You're right," his mother said. "Did she wander
off?"

Pete cupped his hands and called, but there was no
reply. Then all the children began to search through
the house for Sue.

Finally Dolores chuckled. "Well, well, see what I
found here!"

She pointed to a corner of the living room behind
the piano. There was Sue, sitting cross-legged with a

"See what I found here!"

small purse mirror in her hands and looking into her mouth.

"I onna ee ow many teeth I have," she said, finally closing her lips so that she could speak clearly.

The others shook with giggles and Sue emerged from her hiding place. "I guess I really am four years old," she announced soberly. "I only have my baby teeth."

When the Hollisters settled down, all except Ricky went to sleep right away. He was so eager for the next day's trip that it took at least five minutes for him to slip into dreamland. He was up the next morning before anyone else and stood outside Diego's room to be sure of not being left behind.

"Hi!" he said as the older boy came out.

The two cooked their own breakfast and set off on ponies before anyone else was awake. Diego's work included visiting one of the sheep herds and carrying mail and messages to the shepherd in charge. The boy decided to go there first.

After jogging along for an hour the two young riders came to the top of a rocky knoll on which a large herd was scattered about. They dismounted and Diego walked toward a hut where the shepherd stayed.

"Hello, Jim!" he called.

Ricky had not followed Diego. He was busy watching a large dog who had started barking at a great big ram with curled-back horns. The sheep turned and started to run.

Suddenly the angry ram saw Ricky directly in his path. Instead of swerving out of the way, he lowered his head and rushed at the little boy!

CHAPTER 14

A Trick of the Trail

RICKY knew he could not jump out of the way in time to avoid having the ram butt him. What could he do?

"I'll try something!" he thought in desperation.

Just as the huge sheep reached him Ricky leaped into the air and grabbed the ram's horns. He landed with a thud astride the animal's nose, causing a loud *baa* of pain.

"Bravo!" yelled Diego, rushing up and halting the ram.

Back of him was Jim, the tall, blond herder. He shook his head as if he could not believe what he had just seen.

"You're a very brave little fellow," he praised Ricky. Then he turned to the ram. "As for you," he scolded, "you should learn better manners!" and slapped the animal's nose.

Now that the incident was over, Ricky was shaking with fright but he tried not to show it. He patted the big sheep dog who bounded up to him. Jim explained that King Rudy the ram and Rover the dog were not very good friends.

"King Rudy doesn't like to take orders from him," the herdsman said.

"What kind of orders?" Ricky asked.

Jim said that the dog was very good at bringing in the sheep who strayed into the woods or a distance away from the hill. But Rudy never wanted to mind and sometimes tried to jab Rover with his horns.

As Ricky admired Rover, Diego took three letters and a notebook from his pocket and handed them to Jim. The herder wrote several figures in the book, then gave it back.

"Dad will be glad to hear none of your sheep have been rustled," he said.

"I guess we can thank Rover for that," Jim remarked. "He's a great watchdog."

"The other herds have lost quite a few," Diego told him. "Well, Ricky, let's go!"

"Oh please not yet," the little boy begged. "I want to see Rover bring in some sheep."

Jim said this was not usually done until evening but he would put on a little show for Ricky. "I can't get all five hundred of them here now, though," he added with a chuckle.

"Five hundred sheep!" the boy exclaimed. "You take care of all of them by yourself?"

"With Rover. He's worth half a dozen men," Jim said, calling the beautiful dog to him. "He can't count, yet he never stops collecting our sheep until he has every one in. And what's more, if a lamb from a neighbor's flock gets mixed in with ours, he'll chase it away."

"Boy, he's sure smart," Ricky said admiringly.

Jim looked at his dog, who cocked his head awaiting instructions. "Go get Caracul!" he commanded.

There was a slight pause, then Rover bounded off.

"What's a cara—cara—?" Ricky began.

"You wait and see," Diego said, laughing.

Five minutes later they heard barking in a nearby woods and soon a pure black sheep ran out. Rover chased him to his master and the boys.

"Meet our caracul," Jim said. "He's kind of rare."

Ricky had never seen a black sheep and thought his wool very beautiful. He thanked Jim for letting Rover bring him in, then climbed onto his pony. As he and Diego rode off, the ranch boy glanced up at the sun.

The boys set off again.

"It's nine o'clock," he said. "Pete and Pam and Dolores must be starting out for Mystery Mountain."

Diego was right. Pete and Pam had obtained their parents' consent to go but only if Dolores went along. Although younger than the others, she was a seasoned rider and knew the country because of long overnight trips with her father and brother. Jack and Helen Moore had received permission as well.

At this moment the little cavalcade was standing in front of the Bishops' ranch house saying good-by to Mr. and Mrs. Moore. Pete was astride Spot, Pam had Pal, and Dolores was riding Cutie. The Hollisters were wearing their new fur-trimmed cowboy clothes and looked very attractive.

"You'll be careful and stick together, won't you?" Mrs. Moore said.

"We promise," they chorused.

The children chattered gaily as they cantered over the range with Pete in the lead. He had the map from Mesquite's hide-out in his pocket and was following the direction indicated.

Reaching a wooded section with a steep grade, they slowed to a walk. From time to time Pete consulted the map.

They went down one steep gully and up another. The ground was strewn with big boulders, which made the going hard for the horses.

"Can't we take a trail?" Helen asked finally. "I don't care if it takes longer to get to Mystery Mountain."

Pete led them into a steep gulch.

"It's too late to turn back now," Pete replied. "Anyway, I'm afraid we'd miss the directions on the map."

He led them down into a gulch that was so steep the children had to lean far back in their saddles. Halfway to the bottom Helen's horse slipped on a loose stone and fell to his knees. The girl went over his head. Fortunately she landed in a bed of moss.

"Oh dear!" she cried, jumping up. "I hope my horse hasn't broken a leg!"

Dolores quickly dismounted to examine the animal. "No, nothing is broken," she said in relief. "But this is wild country. I've never been here before."

The Moore children suggested that they turn back, but the Hollisters and Dolores urged them to go farther. Mystery Mountain did not seem to be far away now!

"Okay," Jack said finally. "You're better pioneers than we are. Lead on!"

Their horses' hoofs drummed against the sandy ground, leaving little puffs of dust behind them. When they came to an open spot, Dolores reined in and pointed.

"See that tall savine tree over there? It's much higher than the trees around it. I'm sure that's the one on the map."

Eagerly the young riders cantered toward the tree, carefully picking their way across the rough ground. Pam was the first to reach the savine. She held up her hand for the others to stop.

"This must be the landmark," she said, turning in her saddle. "But look over there. We're at the rim of a small canyon."

The others were amazed to find themselves so close to the precipice. They dismounted and led the horses to the edge and looked down into a narrow valley. It was about thirty feet deep and was full of beautiful rock formations.

"Oh, I know what this is!" Dolores exclaimed. "I've heard Daddy call it the Hidden Canyon. Ancient people who lived here used it as a ceremonial place."

"Then it might be a clue to Mystery Mountain!" Pete said, glancing at his sister.

"Has anybody ever explored it?" Pam asked Dolores.

The dark-eyed girl nodded. "A group of high school children had a dig here last summer," she said.

"Look! An old pueblo!"

Jack scratched his head. "A dig? What's that?"

"Part of the fun in living out West," Dolores replied, looking dreamily across the canyon. "There are lots of hidden treasures and buried towns around here. Men from the museum are always hunting for them."

"And kids hunt too?" Jack's eyes widened.

"Sure. That's what we call a dig. The children from Sunrise found the remains of an old pueblo here."

Pete snapped his fingers. "Let's go down and look around!"

Jack and Helen now were as eager as the others. All the children hurried back to the savine tree and tied their horses. Then they worked their way down the canyon wall.

"Oh, I see where people were looking!" Pam cried out, reaching the bottom.

She ran over to a low, square wall of ancient adobe bricks. Most of them were broken or worn smooth.

"The skeleton of an old building," Pete observed.

At this remark Helen looked nervous. "Are there any skeletons of people around, do you think?"

"There may be," Pete answered. "But don't worry. They can't hurt you."

Helen did not reply, but Pam noticed that her friend seemed a little scared. So she took her by the hand and said, "Come on, let's look for a treasure."

The five children worked their way over the old dig until Pete came upon a broken shovel.

"Crickets!" he exclaimed. "I can really use this!"

The broken handle was so short that the boy had a hard time pushing it into the ground. The others wandered about, overturning stones.

Finally Pete stopped and mopped his forehead. "Whew! Anybody want to try this for a while?"

"I do!" his sister volunteered, running to get the shovel. "But I'm going to dig over there." She pointed to a small knoll.

"I'll help you," Dolores offered.

"Me too!" Helen said.

The three girls left the boys, and when they reached the knoll, Pam pushed the shovel deep with her foot.

"Do you suppose this is an old burial place?" Helen asked, looking from one girl to the other a bit fearfully.

"It might be," Dolores replied, as she helped to brush away the loose soil with her hands.

All at once the shovel struck something hard. At first Pam thought it was a rock, and dug around it. Then she reached into the hole. The object was not smooth. Pam took her handkerchief and wiped the earth from it as Dolores and Helen looked on eagerly.

"This feels like—like a face!" Pam gasped.

When Helen heard this she screamed and jumped back.

"A skeleton! Jack! Pete! Come here quick! We found a skeleton!"

By the time the boys had raced over and looked into the hole, Pam was digging furiously.

"It's not a skeleton," she said excitedly. "Help me get it out, Pete!"

"Are there any skeletons around here?"

The brother and sister reached down and pulled up a strange stone object about the size of a football. Pam was the first to realize what it was.

"The head of a stone doll!" she cried out.

Pete whistled. "The ancient dollmakers must have lived here."

"We're on the right trail!" Pete shouted. "Mystery Mountain can't be far away!"

Dolores said something rapidly in Spanish. When the children looked at her, she smiled and added, "We'll tell the arc—arc—"

"Archaeologists?" Pam helped her.

"That's right," the Spanish-American girl said. "The men at the museum in Sunrise are always looking for things like this."

"But first we're going to find Mystery Mountain," Jack said, and the others agreed. Then he suggested, "Let's mark this spot and come back later. We'll go for our horses now."

Pete carried the stone doll head under his arm and led the others back to the wall of the canyon. But halfway up, they were startled by the sound of hoofbeats.

Pete handed the doll head to his sister and scrambled upward to the edge of the slope. With a bewildered look he called down:

"Good night! Our horses. They've run away!"

CHAPTER 15

"Where Is the Map?"

"OUR horses didn't run away! They were untied and chased!" cried Dolores indignantly as she reached the rim of the canyon. "Look over there!"

The children gazed toward their left. A man with a ten-gallon hat was galloping away at breakneck speed.

"Mesquite Mike!" Jack cried, sure that he recognized the cowboy and his horse.

The little group stood stunned for a few minutes. Why had he played such a mean trick on them? And had Willie Boot had anything to do with it?

Dolores tried to be cheerful. "Our horses may come back," she said. "Let's wait and see."

But the animals did not return and the Hollisters wondered how long it would take the children to walk home. A couple of days, probably!

"Oh dear!" Helen said, dropping to the ground and brushing away a tear. "Everything's gone wrong trying to find Mystery Mountain!"

"Don't give up," Pam consoled her. "I have an idea."

"What is it?"

"Everything has gone wrong!"

"Instead of walking home, why don't we wait for someone to rescue us?" she suggested. "In the meantime, we can still look for the mountain."

Everyone thought this was a fine plan. Surely Mr. Vega would come searching for them in his plane when they did not show up at home. The rescue would be easy.

"What time will they expect us at the ranch house?" Helen asked.

"By suppertime," Dolores replied. "But you all might as well make up your minds to spend the night here. The plane couldn't start out until morning."

Suddenly Pete groaned. "What are we going to do for food? Our lunch is still tied on the horses!"

Dolores was quiet a few moments, then she told the others that perhaps she could find some food for them.

"There ought to be corn growing wild," she said. "And there are certain sweet ferns that grow where pine trees do. Boys, you start a fire. Pam and Helen and I will hunt for food."

Pete and Jack said they had no matches with them, but they would try the Indian method of making a fire. First they looked for a stone containing flint but failed to locate one.

"I guess we'll have to use a stick," Pete remarked. "You get some dry shavings, Jack, and I'll sharpen a stick."

First, though, he made a tiny well in a dry piece of tree bark with his penknife. Next he whittled a stick to a fine point. It was just finished when Jack brought some tinder-dry pine needles which he crushed and put into the well.

"Here we go," Pete said.

Holding the stick upright between his palms, with the pointed end in the well, he began twirling it back and forth very fast. Jack got down on the ground and gently blew on the needles.

No sign of a spark after several tries! But the boys did not give up and at last were rewarded. A faint whiff of smoke curled up from the dry needles.

"Hurrah!" Pete cried, twirling the stick even faster.

In a matter of minutes the boys had a fire going. When the girls returned, their arms loaded, they gasped in astonishment.

"I didn't believe you could do it," Dolores exclaimed, laying down a giant cactus.

"We're not such dudes as you think," Jack laughed.

When the food was ready, Pam called out, "What can I serve you? We have:

"Roast Indian Corn
Fern and Berry Salad
Cactus Juice"

"I'll take 'em all and plenty of 'em!" Pete replied.

The picnic party was a great success. When it was over, the children stamped out the fire and prepared to start for Mystery Mountain—or at least what they believed from Mesquite's copy of the map to be Mystery Mountain.

At last a whiff of smoke curled up.

"We can't carry this heavy doll head with us," Pete said. "What say we bury it and come back for it later?"

Pam suggested that they hide it at the foot of the savine tree, so Pete climbed down into Hidden Canyon again to get the broken shovel. When they had buried the stone head, the children set off in high spirits. For an hour they slid down *arroyos* and climbed up and down the wooded hills.

"Ow—ee, my feet," Helen moaned. "Let's stop for a rest, Pete."

"I'm thirsty, anyhow," Jack said. "If I only had a drink of water—"

There was none in sight, however. In a few minutes, Pete said:

"Let's go!"

The children crossed another hill, then started down a long, wooded ravine. Suddenly Helen cried out, "Water! I see water!"

The girl pointed excitedly to a pool at the base of a big rock ahead of them.

"Now I can have my drink!" Jack said eagerly.

He raced ahead, with Dolores at his heels. The boy fell to his knees and was about to scoop up some water in his hands when Dolores yelled:

"Stop! Don't drink that!"

Jack looked at her in astonishment, then followed her pointing finger. Near the pool lay the whitened bones of an animal.

"Stop! Don't drink that!"

"I think this water may be poisoned by something in the ground," Dolores told him. "That animal probably drank some and died."

"Gee and I'm so thirsty I could drink an ocean," Jack said, heaving a long sigh.

"We can't afford to take any chances," the ranch girl said firmly. "We'll find water somewhere."

At this moment a bird came to the pool.

"Oh, we must stop him!" Pam cried. "Don't let him drink the poisoned water!"

"Don't worry," Dolores told her. "If it's bad, he won't touch it."

The children stood stock-still and watched as the bird fluttered around the water's edge. After a moment's hesitation he flew away without drinking any of it.

"You were right, Dolores," Jack said admiringly.

The trek continued, with the trip getting rougher and rougher. Finally Pam asked her brother if he was sure the map indicated this direction.

"Why, yes, but I'll look," Pete said.

He put his hand into his pocket and felt around a moment. Then a strange look came over his face.

"I've lost it!" he confessed sheepishly.

"Lost it!" the others repeated.

Everyone dropped to the ground in disappointment and Pete's face grew red with embarrassment. From here on he would have no idea where to head!

"We're really in a mess," he owned up. "And it's all my fault."

To make matters worse, as Jack looked off among the trees, he saw the pool of poisoned water.

"We've been traveling in a circle," he announced.

All of them felt bad about the failure, yet they did not blame Pete for it. He had done his best to find Mystery Mountain.

But Pete did not feel this way about it and took all the blame. He sat lost in thought. How the boy wished he could do something to make up for his mistake! No solution came to him, and he was interrupted by Dolores' saying:

"Let's hunt for a good spot to spend the night."

"You girls choose it," said Pete, who could not pull himself out of the doldrums.

The three went on a hunt. Pam liked a pine needle bed but Dolores felt that it might be pretty chilly among the trees during the night. Helen suggested the bottom of an *arroyo*. The ranch girl said wild animals often roamed through them after dark. This might not be so safe as another place.

"I guess the open range will be best," she decided.

Dolores picked a spot where the soil was not stony and was fairly comfortable to lie on. The little group found more food and prepared supper. Purple shadows began to settle over the land as dusk came on. Then one by one stars suddenly twinkled brilliantly.

All the children but Pete yawned wearily. Presently they lay down and soon were sound asleep. Pete continued to stare into space. In a little while the moon rose and soon bathed the landscape with its silvery light.

The nearby mountain caps stood out clearly and Pete gazed at one after another of them. A flat-topped peak, not very far away, caught his eye.

"That looks just like the sketch in the Mexican book!" the boy thought excitedly.

Pete continued to stare into space.

Suddenly he wondered if what he now saw was really true. A fairly bright light was moving along the side of the mountain. It stopped traveling presently. As Pete watched, it glowed steadily in the one spot. When ten minutes had gone by, the boy's curiosity got the better of him.

"I'm going over there and find out what's up," he told himself. "Maybe I can learn the secret of Mystery Mountain and the kids won't think I'm such a bonehead after all!" Quietly he got up and set off in the direction of the strange light.

CHAPTER 16

A Scare

BACK at the ranch the Hollisters and the Vegas waited anxiously for Pete, Pam, and Dolores to return. They had eaten supper and were sitting in the patio looking toward the mountains.

Diego was softly strumming his guitar in an effort to ease the nervous tension the families felt. Truchas had come over and wore a worried look.

"The children should have been home long ago," Mrs. Hollister said, a note of fear in her voice. "I'm going to telephone Bishop's Ranch and ask Mrs. Moore whether Helen and Jack have arrived."

Before she had a chance to, Holly exclaimed, "Here they come! I hear their horses!"

Diego stopped strumming and everybody listened to the hoofbeats which sounded in the distance. Presently the dim figures of the animals came into view in a cloud of dust.

"Hurray!" Ricky yelled.

But suddenly gasps went up from the patio as the horses drew nearer.

The saddles were empty!

Diego hurried over and grabbed Spot's bridle. "He's come a long distance," the boy said, noting how the horse was sweating.

Truchas examined the horse further and saw that Spot had thrown his shoe and had sticker burrs on his hock.

"This means bad luck," the old man said gravely. "These stickers grow only where the monster dwells."

"What do you mean by that?" Mr. Hollister demanded, noticing a look of fright come over Diego's face.

Truchas told him of the strange mountain that made noises and said the horse doubtless had come from that direction. Mr. Hollister sighed. This sounded like a fairy tale which he would not worry about. But he was much concerned for the children's safety, nevertheless.

It was Mrs. Vega who relieved the tension. "Dolores is a mighty sensible girl," she remarked, "and her daddy has taught her how to camp overnight in an emergency. Like as not the horses just ran away and we'll have to go fetch the children. If they're not back by morning, we'll go to the burr country, monster or no monster."

"I'll call Bishop's Ranch now," Mrs. Hollister said, and went inside to telephone.

After a brief conversation with Mrs. Moore, she hung up and reported that neither Jack nor Helen had returned.

"But their horses didn't come back," Mrs. Hollister said. "It's very strange. Do you think we'd better notify the police?"

They prayed for the children on the range.

The Vegas, although somewhat worried, said there would be no use to do this because a night search would be nearly impossible.

"Let's not worry any more until tomorrow morning," Truchas said philosophically, starting off for his shack.

After he had gone, Mrs. Hollister took Sue to her room and Holly and Ricky also went to bed. When they said their prayers, they asked that all the children out on the range be taken care of safely during the night and return to them the next day. After everything was quiet, Sue slipped out of her bed and went to where Holly was dozing off.

"Don't worry," she told her sister. "Leave them alone and they'll come home, wagging their tails behind them!"

Holly reached over and kissed the little girl, and Sue quickly climbed into bed with her. Later that evening, when Mrs. Hollister was ready to retire, she went to look at each of her children. Coming to Holly's bed, she found the sisters snuggled close together, with Sue holding one of Holly's pigtails in her chubby hands. Quietly Mrs. Hollister carried the baby of the family back to her own bed.

Morning dawned bright and sunny but since the travelers had not returned, it seemed gloomy to the Hollisters and Vegas. Diego got his father's binoculars, and, climbing to the roof of their barn, scanned the countryside in all directions. The children were not in sight.

"We'll have to act now and act fast," Mr. Hollister said with determination. "Frank, is your plane in shape to start a search?"

"Not quite," Mr. Vega replied nervously. "I'm going to continue repairing it immediately." He hurried to the barn, swung open the door, and set to work feverishly. As he did, he called back to Mr. Hollister, suggesting that he and Diego go searching with Truchas and take the missing children's horses with them.

"I'll scout in the air as soon as I get the propeller and wheel fixed," he promised.

At once Ricky said he wanted to go with his father, and Holly begged to be permitted to join the trip.

Mrs. Hollister, smiling a little sadly, said, "I'm going along too!"

"It's very rough riding out there," Mr. Vega warned her.

"But I'll not stay here while my son and daughter are missing," she told him resolutely.

Mrs. Vega put an arm around Mrs. Hollister's shoulders. "I know how you feel," she said bravely. "Go by all means. I'll stay here and tend to the house. Somebody might telephone with information about the children."

"I want to go too," Sue pleaded, tugging at her mother's hand.

But it was decided she was too small for such a long ride on horseback and would stay at home with Mrs. Vega. When the little girl started to cry, the kindly woman said, "Wouldn't you like to play house with the rabbits?"

Sue dried her eyes, then went to the kitchen to help put breakfast on the table. Twenty minutes later,

They followed the hoofprints.

while Diego and Truchas were saddling and bridling the horses, Mrs. Hollister and Holly helped Mrs. Vega quickly pack sandwiches and tomato juice for the riders.

"I know you want to hurry," she said. "I do hope you'll have good luck."

As they rode in two's across the range, it was not hard to follow the hoofprints that Spot, Pal, and Cutie had made the evening before. But finally they became lost in a maze of cattle marks.

The party rode all morning without stopping. Then Truchas said they must rest the horses.

"We'll eat our lunch while we're waiting," Mrs. Hollister said, although she hated to lose a precious moment.

"There's a nice shady grove of pine trees ahead," Diego said. "Let's go there."

As they approached the trees, Ricky suddenly spurred his horse forward.

"What's the matter?" Holly shouted.

"I see something white," the boy replied without explaining further.

Before the others could catch up to him, he had reined in and hopped off his horse. Excitedly he approached a clump of rabbit brush. Suddenly, from it came a loud rattling noise.

"Be careful!" Diego cried out. "It's a snake!"

Ricky jumped back just in time. The vicious fangs of a rattlesnake struck out toward him, missing the boy's leg by inches.

The child was so startled he could not move. The snake coiled to strike again. Seeing Ricky's danger, Diego leaped from his horse, picked up a stone, and flung it at the rattler. It was a perfect hit and the snake lay still.

"Oh, thank you, Diego," Ricky said. Then he pointed to something white in the rabbit brush. "That's what I wanted you to look at."

Diego reached in and pulled out a narrow piece of white rabbit fur. A few broken stitches were attached to it.

"I'll bet it's off the cowboy suits Pete and Pam have on!" Ricky told him.

"A clue!" Mr. Hollister said happily. "Well, at least we're on the right track."

The group spread out and looked to the left and right as they worked their way slowly up a small hill. When they reached the top of it, Diego pointed excitedly to the valley below.

"People!" he exclaimed.

They were too far away to be recognized but the searchers hoped they were the missing children. If not, at least they might have seen them.

"Come on! Let's get to those people before they disappear!" Mr. Hollister urged.

Truchas mumbled something about burr country and the monster but fortunately Diego did not hear him. The riders went on as fast as they dared. Soon they lost sight of the group in the distance as the make-

"We've found them!"

shift trail took them into a green valley, then through
another patch of woodland.

"I'm afraid they'll be gone," Mrs. Hollister murmured nervously as the minutes ticked away.

Then suddenly there was a clear view ahead. Across
an open stretch of range stood four children. Pam,
Dolores, Helen, and Jack!

"We've found them!" Ricky cried, and gave an
Indian war-whoop call to attract their attention.

The children heard it and came running toward
the riders. When they met, everybody started talking
at once.

"We're so glad you came!"

"How did you know where to find us?"

"What happened to you?"

But the Hollisters' first question was, "Where's
Pete?"

"He's gone," Pam reported sadly. "Pete disappeared
last night and he hasn't come back!"

CHAPTER 17

A Tiny Parachute

"PETE gone! But where?" Mrs. Hollister exclaimed.

"I think he went to find Mystery Mountain," Pam answered, and told how bad her brother had felt about losing the map. "Only he should have been back by this time," she added, tears in her eyes.

Dolores said they had decided to stay in the spot where the group had spent the night, so that Pete could join them. But now they were afraid he was lost.

"Or captured by Mesquite Mike," Jack spoke up. "He's the one who made our horses run away."

"That lazy, good-for-nothing cowboy!" Truchas burst out. "Wait till I see him. I'll—I'll—"

The old man never finished the threat, for at that moment they heard a plane. Looking up, they watched it come nearer.

"It's Dad!" Diego cried.

Mr. Vega evidently spotted the party on the ground, for he dipped the plane's wings in recognition.

"I wish we had some way to tell him Pete's missing," Pam spoke up.

"I know a way," Diego said. "Let's separate so he can count us. Dad will see right away that one is missing."

Quickly the little assembly scattered. Mr. Vega circled the range twice. Then, as if he understood the message, he dipped the wings again.

This time he flew off, going back and forth above each mountain peak. Those below waited tensely to see if he could learn anything about Pete.

Twenty minutes later Mr. Vega came back. The children wondered if he would attempt a landing, but Diego said the ground was too uneven and stony. It would rip the wheels off.

"Oh look!" Ricky cried.

Something white appeared out of the plane window and began to float toward the earth.

"A handkerchief parachute!" Diego exclaimed, as it fluttered closer to the ground. "Dad's sending a message to us!"

"It's going to land right here," Holly cried excitedly.

But just then a sudden breeze caught the little parachute.

"Oh," Ricky moaned, "it's going to blow into the trees."

The handkerchief became snagged in the topmost branches of a tall pine tree and everyone groaned.

"We must get it," Mr. Hollister said.

"I'll climb the tree!" Ricky offered. "Somebody lift me to the first branch."

The lowest limb was twelve feet above the ground, however, and this was not going to be easy. Truchas stepped forward, fingering a lariat which he held in his hands.

"With this," he said, "we can fix that easy," and flung the lariat over the limb. The loop dangled down the other side.

"All set, Ricky." He grinned and tied the noose around the boy's waist. Then he pulled on the other end of the rope, hoisting the lad safely to the limb.

"Neat trick," Diego praised the herder, and everyone clapped.

"Okay, here I go," Ricky said, as he scrambled upward through the branches of the big tree.

Everybody below watched breathlessly as the boy climbed higher and higher. Finally Ricky reached the top branch, at the end of which dangled the parachute.

"Can you reach it?" Mrs. Hollister cried.

"Neat trick!"

"I—I think I can."

Holding on with one arm to the trunk of the tree, Ricky reached out as far as he could, but the parachute was inches from his fingers.

"How will I ever get it?" the boy thought. "If I let go of the trunk, I might fall."

Then an idea came to him. Holding on to the tree trunk with the crook of his arm, Ricky unbuckled his belt and swung it outward with his free hand.

It caught the cords of the handkerchief parachute.

"Nice work!" his father shouted as Ricky pulled the message toward him triumphantly.

He stuck it into his pocket, put his belt back on, and scurried down through the branches.

"Drop into my arms," Mr. Hollister instructed his son.

Ricky hung on to the lowest limb, then let go. *Swish!* He landed safely in his father's arms.

"Let's see the message, dear," Mrs. Hollister said eagerly, and Ricky handed it to her.

The piece of paper was folded into a tiny square and tied with string. When Mrs. Hollister opened it, she gasped in surprise.

"Pete's a prisoner!" she exclaimed.

"Oh no!" cried her children, and tears rolled down their cheeks.

"Read the rest," Mr. Hollister urged, his voice shaky.

His wife read nervously:

"On the far side of the flat-topped mountain I saw three figures. Two of them pulled the third out of sight as I flew

over. It's my guess Pete is a prisoner. I have radioed the police but it will take some time for them to get to the mountain. Do you want to try your luck?"

"Do we!" Mr. Hollister exclaimed.

Quickly mounting the horses, with Jack and Helen riding double, they crossed the range. Truchas led the way, and soon the party began its climb up the closely wooded mountainside. There was no sign of a trail, making the trip very slow.

"Maybe those bad men will take Pete away," Holly worried.

"And we'll never see him again," Ricky said.

"Children," Mrs. Hollister called firmly, "let's hope for the best."

They were riding single file now in a forest of pine and ash. Truchas was in the lead, picking his way among the tall trees, when Pam, directly behind, pulled up to his side.

"Do you think the monster—" she began, but never finished the sentence.

All at once there was a rustling in the woods near them and a frightened deer bolted across their path. The two horses whinnied and reared.

"Whoa!" Truchas shouted, reining in his mount.

But Pam's horse kicked up his heels and dashed forward at breakneck speed. The move was so unexpected that the reins were jerked from the girl's hands. Pam grabbed the animal's mane to keep from falling off.

"Help!" she cried.

"Help!" Pam cried.

By the time Truchas could calm his horse and start to gallop after her, Pam's mount was far ahead, running madly up the steep mountain.

Truchas had nearly caught up, when he noticed a tree with a low-hanging branch directly in the girl's path. It seemed certain that she would be knocked from the saddle!

"Duck!" he yelled.

But Pam had another idea. She wanted to get off the horse! As the branch loomed up, she grabbed it securely with both hands and hung on tightly. The horse galloped away from under her.

"Hang on!" Truchas cried. "I'm coming!"

The herder guided his horse directly beneath the dangling girl and Pam dropped down in front of him on the saddle.

"Oh thank you, Truchas," the girl said in relief.

"Glad I was handy," the old man answered. "Now we'll get your horse."

They galloped up the slope. Spotting the runaway, he yelled "Whoa!" and when it did not stop, Truchas neatly roped him with his lariat.

"There, quiet, boy, quiet!" he said, stroking the horse's nose to calm him.

By this time the others had come up, and after a word of praise to both Pam and Truchas, started to move on.

As Pam was about to put her foot into the stirrup, she noticed a piece of paper half crushed into the pine needles under a nearby tree.

"That's odd," she thought, and walked over to pick it up.

Pam looked at it curiously before realizing it was upside down. When she looked at it the right way, the girl let out a shriek. "Daddy! Mother! Everybody! Look at this!"

As everyone gathered around, Holly said, "It's the lost page from the book about Mystery Mountain!"

"Since Mesquite Mike took it," Jack said, "he must be close by."

"And he dropped this only a short time ago," Mr. Hollister reasoned, seeing that the paper was very clean.

"In that case," said Truchas, "we must be extra careful. That human coyote ain't to be trusted."

The ground over which they now rode was becoming more stony by the minute. And the trees were so close together that a horse could hardly get between.

"We'll have to figure this out," Truchas said, stopping the train of riders. He squinted to his left. "I see daylight over there," the herder told them. "Let's walk in that direction."

Everyone dismounted and hurried toward the open spot. It proved to be a bare section of the far side of Mystery Mountain. Above them loomed a cliff.

All this time they had been chattering but now Diego said, "Listen! I think I hear voices up there!"

"Everybody! Look at this!"

The Hollisters and their friends became quiet, staring upward. A moment later a head appeared over the edge.

"It's Pete!" Pam shrieked.

"Yes, it is," Mrs. Hollister said thankfully. "We've found him!"

Pete put his fingers over his lips to indicate it was not safe for them to be heard. Leaning over, he said in a hoarse whisper:

"Go to the place where there are two big rocks. A secret trail starts there and comes up here."

Mr. Hollister nodded and said with only his lips moving, "Where are the rocks?"

Pete started to give further directions when suddenly a man appeared behind him and clapped a hand over the boy's mouth. Pete was dragged out of sight!

CHAPTER 18

A Mysterious Cave

"WE MUST get to Pete at once!" Mrs. Hollister said anxiously.

"But how?" Pam asked. "He didn't have time to tell us where the big rocks are."

"I think I saw them," Diego spoke up. "They're a little way from where Pam's horse ran off."

Going downhill it did not take the riders long to reach the spot. Just as they arrived, hoofbeats below told them someone else was coming through the woods. A friend? Or Mesquite Mike?

In a minute two horsemen came into view. State troopers!

Ricky rushed over, saying, "How did you get here so fast?"

"Fast?" asked one, introducing himself as Officer Kelly. "We started out early this morning—as soon as we got the message from Mr. Moore."

"Oh," said Diego. "My dad radioed too, but only a couple of hours ago."

The story of Pete's capture was quickly told and everyone was glad to let the officers take the lead up the secret trail. Apparently this would take them to the precipice, but from another direction. Presently the path joined a well-traveled trail leading from the valley below. Diego cried out:

"Sheep have been driven up here!"

The marks were plainly visible and everyone became doubly excited. The missing sheep were probably hidden here!

"Pete must have found them," Mr. Hollister stated. "Mesquite had planned to hold my son a prisoner until the sheep could be safely driven away."

"But where are the sheep?" Ricky asked. "Maybe they've already gone."

No one could answer this, but in a moment the troopers stopped. They had reached a small clearing with a giant overhang of rocks to their right. It looked like an immense auditorium, extending far into the mountainside. As the others halted to look, the riders heard a rumbling sound.

"That's the monster," Truchas said, glancing this way and that to see where the noise was coming from.

There was no sign of a monster, however, and the cavalcade moved on. The clattering of the horses sounded hollow as they went deeper into the dome-like hole in the mountaintop. Here and there openings in the top let in light.

The policemen advanced cautiously, looking in every direction. But it was Ricky who was first to spy anything.

"Horses!" he shouted. "Over there!"

"We give up!"

Tethered to a low bush beside the rock wall stood four horses.

"Two of them are ours!" Jack cried.

"We're nearing the end of our search," Officer Kelly said grimly.

A few yards farther on they heard the *baa* of sheep. The riders urged their horses forward at a gallop. As they rounded a bend in the cavern an amazing sight met their eyes. Pete Hollister was driving a small flock of sheep into the far end.

"All right, all right, we give up!" came muffled cries.

"Pete!" Mrs. Hollister exclaimed as she jumped from her horse and hurried toward her son. "What on earth are you doing?"

The boy was too busy to stop and embrace his mother, but pointed to two figures pinned against the wall by the milling sheep.

All at once Pete saw the two policemen and stopped urging the sheep forward. "Well, what do you know about that?" Officer Kelly said. "Pete, you turned the tables and trapped those two!"

"Let me out of here! Please! Please!" Willie sobbed.

The two officers pushed through the flock and collared the pair as Pete explained that he had tricked Mesquite and Willie into entering the cave and then had captured them.

"I was afraid you wouldn't get here in time, though," he said.

Pete told them that the mean cowboy, with Willie's help, had stolen the sheep and hidden them here until he thought it was safe to bring them out. As he was talking, Dolores climbed from her horse and started to walk among the sheep.

"Here's my lamb!" she cried excitedly, hugging her pet.

When the excitement died down a bit, Pete announced that he had found the Cave of the Dollmakers.

"Come on, I'll show it to you," he said, leading them forward.

While the policemen questioned Mesquite and Willie, Pete led the others through a narrow passage among solid rocks.

On a ledge stood several dolls hewn from stone, and scattered among them were small stone toys which Mr. Hollister said children of long ago used.

"Their faces look just like the doll's head we found in Hidden Canyon," Pam said. "That was a good clue!"

"Oh, Pete, you solved the story of Mystery Mountain!" Helen Moore cried. "How wonderful!"

The dolls were heavy, but each child carried one, along with a toy. Even though they knew these ancient objects belonged to the state, they were happy to have them even a short time.

"And I solved another mystery, too, before Mesquite captured me," Pete said. "I'll show you."

A little distance ahead the growling, gurgling sound they had heard constantly became louder. Finally Pete stopped before a crack in the ground.

"Put your ear to that," he told them.

The children fell to their knees and listened. Far below they could hear the sound of rushing water!

"An underground river!" Diego shouted. "Truchas, that's the monster you've talked about for years!"

The old herder grinned sheepishly. "I guess you're right. Well, I'm sure glad we found out what it was. And now," he added, "Cottonwood Ranch needn't ever suffer again from lack of water. We'll just pipe this monster right down to where he's needed."

He turned around and they all went back to where the policemen were. After voicing surprise over what the Hollisters had found, Officer Kelly said, "Mesquite has admitted everything. The ranchers won't be bothered by him any more. As for Willie, I hope he'll get some sense now and play with nice boys and girls instead of running around with rustlin' cowboys!"

"I will! I will!" Willie promised.

The conversation was interrupted by the sound of an airplane, and everyone dashed from the cavern to see if it was Mr. Vega's. It was, and when he saw Pete, the officers, their prisoner, and the missing sheep he dipped his wings over and over and so fast that it made everyone laugh.

What excitement there was at Cottonwood Ranch the next night! Helen and Jack Moore, with their parents, had come over for the evening. After a gay celebration at dinner, the Vegas got out their instruments and played the liveliest music the children had ever heard.

The old herder grinned foolishly.

In the middle of it the telephone rang and Mr. Vega went to answer it. He returned a few minutes later with a broad smile.

"Good news," he said. "In appreciation of the Hollister and the Moore children finding the ancient dolls and toys, our state is going to give each family one. Take your pick!"

There was a little discussion but each group finally decided on one. Then Pam said to her brothers and sisters:

"Let's give ours to the Shoreham Museum."

"That would be very nice," said Mrs. Vega. "With it could be a card reading:

"Donated by the Happy Hollisters,
Who Found This on Mystery Mountain."

"We'll do that," Pete agreed.

Sue, who felt she had had no part in solving the mystery, suddenly spoke up in a loud voice. "Mr. Vega, I want to take home a gift from Cottonwood Ranch."

"What would you like to have?" he asked.

Without a second's hesitation, the little girl cried, "A burro! I want Sunday!"

Everyone rocked with laughter at the request and never dreamed that it would be granted. But to the others' surprise Mr. Vega said, "You shall have our dear Domingo."

"Oh, thank you!" Sue said, hugging him. "Then every week will start right in our house. I'll ride Sunday to church."

DON'T MISS A SINGLE ADVENTURE —
COLLECT ALL 33 VOLUMES OF
THE HAPPY HOLLISTERS BY JERRY WEST!

1) The Happy Hollisters
2) The Happy Hollisters on a River Trip
3) The Happy Hollisters at Sea Gull Beach
4) The Happy Hollisters and the Indian Treasure
5) The Happy Hollisters at Mystery Mountain
6) The Happy Hollisters at Snowflake Camp
7) The Happy Hollisters and the Trading Post Mystery
8) The Happy Hollisters at Circus Island
9) The Happy Hollisters and the Secret Fort
10) The Happy Hollisters and the Merry-Go-Round Mystery
11) The Happy Hollisters at Pony Hill Farm
12) The Happy Hollisters and the Old Clipper Ship
13) The Happy Hollisters at Lizard Cove
14) The Happy Hollisters and the Scarecrow Mystery
15) The Happy Hollisters and the Mystery of the Totem Faces
16) The Happy Hollisters and the Ice Carnival Mystery
17) The Happy Hollisters and the Mystery in Skyscraper City
18) The Happy Hollisters and the Mystery of the Little Mermaid
19) The Happy Hollisters and the Mystery at Missile Town
20) The Happy Hollisters and the Cowboy Mystery
21) The Happy Hollisters and the Haunted House Mystery
22) The Happy Hollisters and the Secret of the Lucky Coins
23) The Happy Hollisters and the Castle Rock Mystery
24) The Happy Hollisters and the Cuckoo Clock Mystery
25) The Happy Hollisters and the Swiss Echo Mystery
26) The Happy Hollisters and the Sea Turtle Mystery
27) The Happy Hollisters and the Punch and Judy Mystery
28) The Happy Hollisters and the Whistle-Pig Mystery
29) The Happy Hollisters and the Ghost Horse Mystery
30) The Happy Hollisters and the Mystery of the Golden Witch
31) The Happy Hollisters and the Mystery of the Mexican Idol
32) The Happy Hollisters and the Monster Mystery
33) The Happy Hollisters and the Mystery of the Midnight Trolls

For more information about *The Happy Hollisters*,
visit www.TheHappyHollisters.com

Made in the USA
Las Vegas, NV
30 August 2023

76851296R00105